JEALOUS LOVE

Lee has given Des Palmer up because he is insanely jealous. When she goes out with Roy, Des stabs him. Roy dies from the wound, but Des pleads that Lee had provoked him by going out with Roy almost on the eve of their wedding. He is sentenced to four years in prison, and when he is released Lee is terrified. She is now happily married to Brett and is afraid that Des will harm him or herself. Her suspicions are confirmed when she discovers Des is keeping a watch on her . . .

HILDA PERRY

JEALOUS LOVE

Complete and Unabridged

LINFORD
Leicester

First published in Great Britain in 1982

First Linford Edition
published 2001

British Library CIP Data

Perry, Hilda
    Jealous love.—Large print ed.—
    Linford romance library
    1. Love stories
    2. Large type books
    I. Title
    823.9'14 [F]

    ISBN 0–7089–5985–7

Published by
F. A. Thorpe (Publishing)
Anstey, Leicestershire

Set by Words & Graphics Ltd.
Anstey, Leicestershire
Printed and bound in Great Britain by
T. J. International Ltd., Padstow, Cornwall

This book is printed on acid-free paper

1

At first Lee Foster had found it rather flattering to have a young man who loved her so much he couldn't bear her to look at another. His name was Des Palmer and almost as soon as he'd come to work at Lawley's he'd taken a fancy to Lee and she was really thrilled when he asked for a date.

He worked in the accounts department and she often had to go into that department to check on certain accounts and that was how she got to know him well.

He lost no time in letting her know how deeply he felt for her and took her home to meet his parents. They lived in an old type house, standing in its own grounds just on the outskirts of the town and Lee had taken to them right away.

Within a few months of their first

date Des wanted to get engaged and she felt she was being swept off her feet. They went house hunting and he was planning for them to be married as soon as possible.

Lee's family liked him and everything was fine except that she found herself afraid to talk to another man when Des was around. If he saw her talking to someone else he would come up immediately, be rather rude to the other man until he took the hint and walked away, and then he would want to know why she had encouraged him.

'I haven't encouraged him at all,' she would protest. 'I was simply being friendly. This is a party.'

'You belong to me,' he would say, with a dark look on his face, and after a time this sort of behaviour began to worry her. She didn't like not being able to talk to anyone else, feeling Des's eyes upon her, making her feel uncomfortable.

And his jealousy began to increase as time went on. He not only hated her to be friends with young men, it extended to members of her own sex. He didn't want her to continue seeing Jean with whom she had been friends as long as she could remember.

'Jean is a special friend,' she told Des. 'I could never stop seeing Jean.'

'Not even for me?'

'No, not even for you, Des. At the rate you are going I won't have a friend in the world. You have objected to my speaking to any of the men I know and now you're objecting to my girl friends.'

'It's only because I love you and don't want to share you with anyone else,' he assured her. 'I live just for you, and I want you to live just for me.'

He got extremely angry when she said that was silly. That they could still be in love and yet have friends of whom they were fond.

She worried over his attitude and yet he had a way of making her forget his jealousy for when he kissed her and made love to her he simply carried her away and she told herself that once they were married everything would be fine. He was simply afraid of losing her.

She couldn't imagine why he had to be so afraid that she might prefer someone else for he was an extremely handsome man. He had thick dark hair, dark brown eyes, was tall and always well dressed. He had a beautiful speaking voice and she loved everything about him and told him so regularly so that he would have no need to be afraid that when she spoke to anyone else she was forgetting him.

When they went house hunting he wanted to buy a house way out of town, far away from her people and Lee had always been fond of her family. She knew she would want to call and see them as often as she could after she was married. This annoyed Des.

'When we marry we want to be entirely alone. No interference from anyone.'

'But my family won't interfere, Des. They'll be thrilled we're married and have a home of our own and they'll come and visit and we shall want to visit them.'

'And before you know where you are they'll start telling you how to run your life. No, Lee, we live right away from your family and mine.'

That was when Lee started to put her foot down. She'd had enough of Des's possessiveness. 'I do not intend to cut myself away from my friends and my family when I get married, Des,' she declared.

'You want to start a new life, don't you? Can't you understand that I want you to myself? I don't want to share you.'

'I'm not asking to live next door to my family,' she argued. 'But I can't see why we have to live miles away from them to make it difficult for me to go and see them as often as I'd like. I shall work for a time after we're married so will have little time to spare and I'd like to think my parents lived not too far away for me to travel and see them.'

'There won't be any need for you to

work after we're married, Lee.'

'But I'd be bored to tears all day at home.'

'You mean you'd miss all the men you work with,' he said, scornfully. 'You like to be popular with everyone you work with, don't you?'

'I've never looked at it like that,' she retorted. 'I just look on it as being friendly and sociable with people. I've always got on well with people until I met you and now I find myself wondering if I ought to speak to men at work in case you're going to be displeased about it.'

'I don't go round talking to all the girls.'

He didn't, now she came to think of it. He kept himself very much to himself. People liked him, but he didn't give them the chance to know him more than at a superficial level.

She was very quiet and he began to worry in case he had offended her. 'I'm sorry, you're angry with me, Lee,' he said. 'It's only because I love you so

6

much that I'm scared of losing you.'

'But I've told you, Des, you have no need to be scared of losing me. I love you.'

But after a time, arguments like this, always ending with him declaring once again that he only wanted her to be interested in him, and she herself declaring that he needn't be afraid of losing her, began to be so repetitive she found that her insistence that she loved him was beginning to be untrue. She didn't want to be with someone who hated her to be interested only in him. It was selfish and he would make her life a hell through his jealousy.

She made up her mind to finish with him. It was the only thing to do. She didn't want to, really, because she knew if he wasn't so obssessed with the idea that she belonged just to him alone, she could love him very much.

It was going to be difficult to end their affair because there were her people and his to think of. They had had a nice engagement party, received lots of engagement presents and now she was going to call the whole thing off, but something told her she had to. Exciting as it had been in the first place to have a fiancé who wanted to possess her completely, she no longer found she wanted to be regarded as someone's exclusive property.

She had known it wouldn't be easy, but had not been at all prepared for Des's reaction when she plucked up the courage to tell him she didn't want to see him again.

In the beginning he was furiously angry with her. He said he knew she didn't mean it and was only telling him that to upset him, but she was determined to end this affair.

'I do mean it, Des,' she told him. 'You are too jealous for my liking. I'm the type who likes to be friends with other people and you don't like that, so we have to finish.'

He threatened her then, and that frightened her. 'If I can't have you I'll see that no else does,' he said.

She felt a cold shiver go through her and knew even more that she had to finish with a man like that. To threaten her if she finished with him was the last straw. She had to get away from him. He would ruin her life.

'You're talking silly,' she said, 'and it's cowardly to threaten me because I want to finish with you. You can't scare me into marrying you.'

After that he'd cried and begged her, pleaded with her not to give him up, but she had to harden her heart because he had promised over and over again that he'd stop being jealous, but he just couldn't help himself.

'Des, it's your own fault that I'm ending our engagement,' she said, handing back his ring. 'I loved you very much and wanted to marry you, but not any more. I won't be possessed by you, and you alone. I need my family, and I need my friends. I'm afraid I don't love you enough to give them all up for you.'

He refused to take the ring but she

popped it into his pocket and then left him. They were at his home, and there was no one else in, so she left the house and ran up the drive to catch a bus home. Des ran after her and struggled with her. Tears streamed down his face as he begged her to give him just one more chance but Lee had steeled herself to finish with him and wouldn't be talked out of it.

She struggled to free herself, reached the end of the drive and ran along the street. A bus was coming and, without waiting to see if it was the one she wanted, she got on it when it stopped and saw Des looking after her like a wild man. She went upstairs on the bus to avoid the curious looks of the passengers who had seen her chasing away from him.

The tears in her eyes were because she hated to hurt anyone, and yet she felt relieved that she'd had the courage to break off the engagement. Her friends at work wouldn't be surprised because they'd discovered that she wasn't happy about her engagement to Des, and they too, realised that he was unreasonably jealous.

It would be awkward, she supposed, having to go to work at the same place as Des, but it would be stupid of her to give up a good job just because she had broken off her engagement. And the fact that she was thinking more about how she would feel working at the same place as Des instead of how she was going to get on without him was proof to her that he, himself, had killed any love she had for him.

He didn't turn up for work the next day, but she supposed he would soon get over their split up. To a man like Des it would be a blow to his pride more than anything else. He obviously wanted to be the main person in his girl's estimation and to find that she didn't intend to allow him to be that, would affect his pride.

As soon as she arrived at work she went into the sales department to find her friend Jean who was a fresh-faced

11

blonde, taller and bigger than the dark petite Lee. When Lee told her the engagement was off Jean looked at her for a moment, quite seriously, and then commented, 'You don't look heart-broken.'

'No,' said Lee. 'I'm not. I'm just relieved that at last I've had the courage to end something that could only lead to misery for me. I've heard of jealous, possessive husbands and have no intention of being the wife of such a man.'

'Tell you what,' said Jean, 'I've met a young man called Dave and he and his mate are absolutely mad on fishing. They asked if I could find another girl for this Sunday and suggested we went out in a foursome to fish by the riverside. Sounds romantic, doesn't it?' she grinned. 'I'd be bored to tears on my own, but it would be great if you'd come along.'

'Well, why not?' said Lee. 'I've nothing else to do.'

The next day Jean sought her out and

said she'd told her friend, Dave, and he and his friend Roy wanted to make an early start on Sunday morning. 'They said they'd book a meal at the Fieldhouse. I believe they do lovely Sunday mid-day meals,' said Jean.

And so Lee found herself with something to look forward to for Sunday. It sounded as if it could be okay if the weather remained fine. She and Jean would never be bored in each other's company, and they could take a walk along the riverside while the men sat fishing. It sounded an ideal way to spend a day in the country.

She heard that Des had turned up for work this morning and when he came to speak to her she felt glad. Once they'd got used to the idea that there was nothing serious between them it wouldn't be awkward working at the same place with him after all.

He had a dark brooding look on his face which she recognised. He always looked like that when he was angry with her. 'So you've told everyone the engagement is off,' he remarked.

'I've told my friends, naturally,' she replied. 'They'd learn sooner or later.'

'You can't mean to carry on with this,' he went on. 'You couldn't just forget me like that.'

'Des, you know I wouldn't be suitable for you, I'm far too independent,' she tried to reason with him.

'You're the one I want,' he persisted. 'You're driving me mad, do you know that?'

'You'll get over it,' she said.

'Look, it doesn't have to be final, does it? We can be friends. Mother thought you might like to come round on Sunday. We could talk things over in a calmer frame of mind.'

'Oh, I'm sorry, Des. I'm going out with Jean on Sunday. On a fishing trip, would you believe it?'

'Where?' he asked, unbelievingly.

She told him and he said, 'You'll be bored to tears. Who else is going?'

'A couple of fellows Jean knows. They needed another to make up a foursome, and then we'll be having a meal at the Fieldhouse so it should make a nice change.'

'I can't see you in a pub on a Sunday lunch time with a lot of fishermen. The Fieldhouse is a proper meeting house for men who go fishing on a Sunday.'

'Well there's nothing wrong with that, is there?'

'It's not your scene at all. Change your mind and come to our place on Sunday. You're fond of my folks, aren't you?'

'I want to make a clean break, Des,' she said. 'We've had arguments before and I've always given in to you because you've promised to change, but you'll never change. I'm glad I know that we're not suited now before it's too late. We could have been married before I discovered that we didn't suit each other.'

Fortunately at that moment the phone rang and she was called to attend to an enquiry so Des had to leave her.

She supposed that he would make

other attempts to get her to make it up with him but hoped that when he saw that it was no use he would give up.

She found herself looking forward to Sunday. Jean said that they would call and pick her up around six o'clock in the morning.

'Six o'clock!' she exclaimed. 'We must be mad to get up at that time when we have the chance to get a lie in.'

'Fishermen always start early,' grinned Jean.

And so Lee was ready and waiting when they came for her. The young men were about the same age as themselves, just in their twenties. Jean's boy was named Dave and his friend Roy was very young looking with a fresh complexion and unruly fair hair. Very boyish after Des, but Lee liked him. He laughed heartily at the mildest joke and they all set off light-heartedly, the boys telling how many fish they hoped to catch, and how successful they'd been in the past.

As the day had started off rather

chilly they set off in warm woollies over their clothes and were able to shed them as the day went on. By mid morning it was absolutely beautiful, the sun shining gloriously, and Jean and Lee walked beside the river thoroughly enjoying being out in the country after being tied in the office all through the week. They found all sorts of things to talk about, and Lee told Jean of all the stupid jealousies which had spoiled her relationship with Des.

'You've done the best thing giving him up now,' said Jean. 'They never change, that sort.'

'I actually liked his possessiveness at first. I thought it showed how much he loved me, and I didn't think he meant it to be taken all that seriously, that it was just a way of letting me see I was his girl. At times his love making was a bit savage, that worried me too. I was determined not to let him have the privileges of a married man before marriage.'

'All the girls envied you when he

asked you to go out with him. I thought he was smashing, myself,' said Jean.

Lee laughed. 'Did you?'

'I must confess I find him very attractive, but there are times when he has that deep brooding look in his eyes. It could give you a thrill of excitement, or fear.'

'I've never been afraid of him. I wouldn't have gone with him if I'd been afraid of him, but he did say that if he couldn't have me no one else would. That sounded like a threat.'

'Nasty thing. Trying to intimidate you.'

'I don't suppose he meant it. He cried afterwards and begged me to think again and I very nearly did. But he's done that before and I've made up a quarrel thinking he'd be different but it seems to me that he can't change his nature.'

They called into a small village store and bought some ice cream which they took back to Dave and Roy.

'Any luck?' asked Jean.

'No,' said Dave, but he didn't seem to mind.

'I can't imagine how you can sit there for hours on the off chance of catching a fish and when you catch one you throw it back again.'

'Oh, well, girls wouldn't understand,' said Roy, scornfully. 'It's the sport.'

Jean made a grab for his hair as he sat there on the bank and gave it a good roughing up. There was lots of laughter and then he told her to give up. 'You're frightening the fish away,' he said. He patted the grassy bank at the side of him and invited Lee to sit by him. 'But be quiet,' he said.

Jean sat beside Dave and the four of them were eating their ice cream when suddenly Roy got excited. 'I've got a bite,' he exclaimed.

The next few minutes were wonderful as he played the fish and eventually caught it and brought it to shore in a net. They weighed the fish, made a note of it, and allowed it to remain in the water though in the net.

Dave had a catch shortly afterwards but it was just a tiny fish which wasn't worth weighing and he let it go back into the river again immediately.

The sun had caught Roy's fair skin and his face was a rosy red after only a few hours of sitting by the riverside. 'They'll think you've been away for a holiday when you go to work tomorrow,' said Lee.

'It's a nuisance being fair-skinned,' he grinned. 'I have to keep out of the sun altogether when it gets very hot.'

They had brought thermos flasks and after a time the girls poured cups of coffee and the young men said they were hungry, but Jean reminded them that they'd booked a meal at the Fieldhouse. 'You'll spoil your appetite if you start eating now,' she told them.

'We had an early breakfast, don't forget,' said Dave. 'I'm starving.'

By lunch time they'd had enough of fishing. They let the fish in the net go back into the river and began packing up to go and get something to eat.

'We'll go for a run afterwards,' said Dave. 'That suit you, girls?'

'Oh, yes, fine,' they said, enthusiastically.

They packed all their fishing tackle away in the boot of the car. They had only come in one car which was Dave's, a Rover with plenty of room in it. It wasn't his, actually, it belonged to his firm, but he said he was allowed to use it for his own purposes.

They all got into the car and Lee knew she was going to enjoy her lunch; she was simply dying for it.

'I'll say one thing for being in the country,' she said. 'It gives you an appetite.'

'Yes, I could eat a horse,' confessed Roy. 'I hope they don't keep us waiting when we get there. It's one o'clock and that's the time we booked.'

Lee was in the back of the car with Roy and she said, 'Do you come fishing most Sundays?'

'I've only just started,' he said. 'Dave got me interested.'

'There's nothing like getting up at the crack of dawn and being down by the riverside to see the sun come up,' said Dave. 'Makes you meditate,' he went on, 'but it's impossible when you've got a couple of girls with you, they distract your attention.'

'I like that!' cried Jean. 'We fetched ice cream for you, poured your coffee and kept extremely quiet when you told us to.'

Dave laughed, he was only teasing, and they all knew that. Lee thought they were smashing boys, so easy to talk to and there were no undercurrents of uneasiness like those she felt when she was with Des.

The lovely weather had fetched crowds out and when they reached the Fieldhouse it was almost impossible to find a spot to park the car. Young couples were sitting in the gardens having a drink and there was quite a holiday atmosphere in the air.

The boys asked the girls what they'd like to drink and then Dave went off to order the drinks and Roy went in search of the receptionist to see how long they would have to wait for their table to be ready.

'See if you can find some seats out here while we're waiting,' said Dave. 'I doubt if there are any available. We'll sit over on that wall if there aren't.'

The receptionist was just coming along to tell a nearby group that their meal was ready to be served and Jean cried, 'How about that then? Just right,' and they both dived to take possession of their seats.

They arranged four chairs round a small table, waiting for the boys to join them and Jean said, 'Glad you came, Lee?'

'Yes, it's been great. Of course the weather makes a lot of difference doesn't it?'

'Do you like Roy?'

'Yes. He seems very young though. I suppose he's older than I am and yet he seems very boyish to me. It's because I've been used to Des who's over thirty.'

'Well, speak of the devil,' said Jean, 'Guess who's sitting over there all on his own?'

'Not Des?' gasped Lee. 'Where?'

'On that seat by the big tree, and he's got his beady eyes on you, Lee.'

At that moment Roy came along with Dave and they were bringing drinks for the girls as well as themselves.

Lee tried to drag her gaze away from Des. She didn't like the look on his face. Why on earth had she told him they were coming here? It was no accident that he had appeared to spoil her day. He'd told her that if he couldn't have her he would see that no one else did and she felt horribly afraid, although she told herself he couldn't do much in a crowded place like this.

'What's wrong, Lee?' asked Roy. 'You look as if you've seen a ghost.'

'Well don't look round,' said Jean. 'Behind you sitting by that old tree is Lee's ex-fiancé. She gave him up a few days ago and it looks as if he's deliberately come here for she happened to tell him she would be lunching here at the Fieldhouse.'

'You think he intends to make trouble?' asked Roy.

'I don't know,' said Lee. 'I gave him up because he was very possessive and jealous. He hated me to talk to any other men. And he threatened that if he couldn't have me no one else would.'

'If he's come to make trouble for you, Lee,' said Dave, 'He's come to the wrong chaps. Roy is an expert at judo, and I've done a bit of boxing in my time. It would be two against one, anyway.'

'He wouldn't cause trouble in a crowded place like this, surely,' said Lee.

'You never know with some chaps,' said Dave. 'Especially when they've had a drink or two.'

Both young men sat themselves down with their drinks and then Lee's heart started to thump when Des sauntered over to them.

'Hello, Lee,' he said. 'Hello, Jean. Going to introduce me to your friends?'

Lee was feeling a little breathless. 'You know Jean. And this is Dave, and this is Roy.'

'Pleased to meet you,' he nodded to the two young men, but Lee could see that he was not at all pleased. 'I believe you're going in for a meal.'

'That's right,' said Dave. 'Sorry we can't invite you to join us we've already ordered.'

'That's all right,' he said. 'Did you catch any fish?'

'Only a couple,' they laughed, 'but it's been a lovely morning for sitting by the river. Gives you a good appetite.'

Roy put his arm across Lee's shoulders in a friendly fashion and she saw Des's expression at the action. If looks could have killed Roy would have dropped dead on the spot.

They spoke about the weather, how good it was and had brought people out of doors. They were just making conversation in a friendly fashion and it was a relief to Lee when she saw the receptionist come to them to tell them their meal was ready to be served. They rose from their seats. 'Sorry we have to go,' said Dave, 'but you know how it is.'

'Don't go for a minute I want to talk to you, Lee,' said Des.

'Oh, not now,' she said. 'Another time, if you must.'

'Now,' he insisted, and went to take her wrist, but Roy held out his hand to take hers at the same time. 'You heard,' he said. 'Some other time.'

'There won't be another time,' said Des, and quick as a flash he produced a flick knife. It may have been intended for Lee, but Roy shielded her and the knife plunged into him.

Lee screamed and screamed as she saw Roy go down. She would never forget the look of bewilderment and shock on his face as he sank to the ground. Before Des could use the knife again he was seized by Dave and a couple of young men nearby. They overpowered him and took the knife from him while Lee knelt beside Roy and sobbed.

2

Life would never be the same again, thought Lee. And she would never feel the same again. The weeks following that Sunday outing had been like a nightmare. There had been the police questions, the court case, and worst of all the horror of knowing that a young man, full of life and happiness, had died because she'd gone out with him that day.

She would never forget the look in Roy's eyes as he lay there after the stabbing. He had died before the ambulance arrived. Sometimes now Lee could hear screams in her head and knew they were the screams she had given over and over, crying, 'No, oh, no!' as she'd watched a life ebb away.

He'd done no harm to anyone and neither had she, and yet the papers had not been very kind in their comments about her. The reporters had seemed to have more sympathy with Des Palmer than his victim, and the reports insinuated that she was very much to blame for what had happened.

Des had been led to kill in a fit of jealousy over a girl who, a few days before being seen at the pub with another young man had been with Des, the man to whom she was engaged. She had been house-hunting with him, led him to believe the wedding would take place almost immediately and then she'd finished with him and had gone out with another young man, taunting him by telling him about the outing and where they were going.

It hadn't been like that at all, but that was how it was reported, and stress seemed to be put on the fact that she had been drinking in a pub at Sunday lunch time which made her seem rather cheap, she thought. She wasn't in the habit of going into pubs drinking, it was only while they had been waiting for their meal, and that wasn't mentioned.

It was no use her trying to put her side of the case forward. Des had a very good solicitor who told how Lee had often made her fiancé jealous by paying attention to other men even before she'd broken off the engagement. Of course this was Des's story and he made her look a real nasty type. He had been very quiet all through the trial. He was dark and handsome, well spoken, and people had pitied him. Lee was to blame. She had deliberately made him jealous. He had been out of his mind at the time and so the verdict was manslaughter and he was given four years. Lee had hardly known Roy and yet she knew she'd never forget him. Never forget the blue eyes that had looked into hers after he'd been stabbed. More surprised than afraid.

She had been so upset it had been impossible to go to work and she felt she couldn't face people, either, after the newspaper reports which made her look like a heartless young person who had driven her fiancé to murder, but her family and friends stood by her, though it didn't stop Lee feeling that she never wanted to go out and mix with people again. It had been a traumatic experience for her.

She couldn't feel sorry for Des Palmer. He was wicked and cruel to have taken Roy's life. He wrote to her from prison but she didn't answer his letters. He was begging for forgiveness now and she remembered how contrite he had always been after a row and would beg her to forgive him. She'd never dreamt that he could go as far as killing someone in his jealousy even though he had threatened that he would not let anyone else have her if he couldn't. Now the thought persisted that he might be planning to kill her when he came out of prison if she refused to agree to being his girl again. He would behave quietly and correctly in prison, she was sure, and she knew that very often prisoners were set free earlier because of good behaviour. She supposed she ought to get right away, perhaps out of the country, so that he'd never be able to find her. She could never feel at ease if she knew he was free to attack again.

She had not been in a fit state to go to work and her parents had been very concerned over her. They wouldn't insist that she went to the office, but felt it was the best thing she could do. She needed to lose herself in her work for a few hours every day at least.

Her boss, Mel Lawley, son of the founder of Lawleys, had written to ask her when she would be returning. He had put someone temporarily in her place but told her he wanted her back at work as soon as possible. She had replied that at the moment she felt she couldn't face all those people at work who would have read all about her in the paper.

Her mother was delighted when one day Mel Lawley came to see Lee. He was shocked at the change in her. She had been a pretty vivacious young girl, but she had lost a lot of weight, looked pale and terribly unhappy and didn't want to talk.

He lost no time in being sympathetic towards her. He told her that tragedies were happening all the time these days and other people rose above them and didn't let them ruin their lives. 'You'll do no good at all sitting at home going through it all over and over again in your mind. Get yourself involved in work and forget it.'

He didn't leave her home without a promise from her that she would return to work. 'You can work in my office for a time. I'll keep you busy and keep an eye on you at the same time,' he said. 'I know you will feel everyone will be discussing what happened, and it's only natural that they should do so, but you have got to forget your involvement in it. Des Palmer has spoilt his own life. You mustn't let him spoil yours.'

It was the fact that Mel Lawley didn't seem to be blaming her for the tragedy, but put the blame entirely on Des, that made her agree to return to work the following day.

And it was not the terrible ordeal she had expected meeting all these people who knew her and what had happened. She went straight to Mel's office and people who saw her on the way gave her a cheery greeting and asked if she was feeling better now. She suspected that Mel had given instructions to the staff not to mention the case to her for no one did. Not even Jean. It was a small firm and there was a good atmosphere amongst the staff.

She was extremely grateful to Mel for she realised now that it was best for her to get back to the office and lose herself in her work. There was no one more conscientious than she for she found no other interest in life now. Mel did keep an eye on her and saw that she began to look less unhappy, but that spontaneous laugh of hers and ready smile had almost disappeared. She made no arrangements to go out with anyone, going straight home from work and staying there until it was time to go back to the office again.

'Where did you go last night?' Mel would ask, quite often, and always it was the same reply, that she didn't go anywhere.

'You're being very stupid, Lee,' he told her. 'Come and spend the week-end with me and Sandra. You'll love our children, they're little darlings,' and from his smile she gathered they were more like little rogues than darlings.

'It's very kind of you . . . ' she began, and he became impatient with her. 'But you're not going to accept, are you? Come on, Lee, pull yourself together. I insist that you come and spend the week-end with us.'

Well, there was no harm in spending the week-end with her boss and his family so she accepted the offer and he called for her on the Saturday morning. She had packed a small week-end case, not expecting to need much in the way of clothes, and was greeted warmly by Sandra. 'It's so nice to have another adult to talk to,' she said. 'I'm tied up with the little ones so much.'

Lee gathered that Mel had been thinking about Sandra as well as herself, knowing that his wife might welcome some young company.

They were adorable little children to be tied up with, thought Lee. There was baby Michael, a few months old, little Paul four years old, and Katie, a very grown up, in her own opinion, seven-year-old. The Lawleys lived in a smart house on the outskirts of the town. It was almost like being in the country and yet in a few minutes by car they could reach a modern shopping-centre where Sandra could get anything she wanted.

'We're going to a dinner-dance this evening, Lee,' said Sandra. 'Mel did mention it didn't he?'

'No, he didn't, but I don't mind baby-sitting at all.'

'You're not baby-sitting,' exclaimed Sandra. 'Fancy Mel not telling you! His mother is coming to baby-sit for us.'

Lee was quite dismayed. 'I can't come,' she said. 'I haven't an evening gown with me.'

'That's no problem,' said Sandra. 'I can lend you one of mine.'

They would listen to no arguments. Mel was so determined to get Lee to go out and mix with people again socially, as well as at work, that she was quite sure he had arranged this outing purposely and hadn't said anything about it knowing she would probably have refused to stay the week-end with his family if he had.

Sandra was quite a petite young woman, the same as Lee, in spite of the fact that she was the mother of three children, so there was no problem about her gowns fitting Lee. They went into her bedroom and there was a whole wardrobe of dresses to choose from.

Lee chose a cream bouclé which fell in folds to the floor and was expertly cut to show her figure to perfection. She needn't have worried herself being odd one out this evening for Mel announced that his cousin was coming to make up a foursome. His name was Brett Lawley. His father and Mel's were brothers.

Lee wasn't happy about this arrangement for it seemed obvious that they were trying to get her fixed up with a young man.

When he arrived she hoped he wouldn't be disappointed with the partner chosen for him for he was a very striking-looking young man. As handsome as Des Palmer, but although he had a very serious air about him, did not have the same dark brooding look as Des had.

He was pleasant enough but not pushing, and they set off to spend an evening at Keynton Hall, a large mansion that had been made into a hotel without spoiling the old world atmosphere of the place.

Mel and Sandra did most of the talking but they were good conversationalists so there was no need for Brett and Lee to feel that they had to say much. There were times when Brett did break in to contradict in a friendly way something Mel had said and they would argue round the point which led sometimes to Mel giving in and admitting that Brett could be right. 'I can't go against the expert,' he said once to Lee. 'You see Brett is a very brilliant economist and administrator. He is employed by one of the greatest engineering firms in this area.'

Brett had looked rather amused at Mel's description of himself and said, 'I'm not brilliant enough to solve some of the economic problems we have to face today, unfortunately.'

Lee had known before Mel told her that his cousin had a responsible position. That he was a man to be respected. There was something about him, and yet he didn't have an arrogant air, or give the impression that he was a man out of the ordinary.

They finished their delightful meal. The dinner wine had put a little colour into Lee's face and her eyes sparkled. She was beginning to enjoy herself though she was quite shy when Brett asked her to dance. But it was only since she had finished her affair with Des with such tragic consequences that she had become so withdrawn. That experience had changed her completely for at one time she was known for her gaiety at parties. Mel was right to try and get her back to living normally, she admitted, for she would have ended up as a recluse if he hadn't taken her in hand, and that was stupid when she was only in her early twenties. She had a good many years before her and ought to enjoy her life as before.

By the end of the evening she and Brett were on quite friendly terms. They danced well together, and although he might hold a responsible position and was looked up to at work, he didn't mind letting his hair down and moving his body to the modern dance rhythms. 'He must be at least ten years older than I am,' she told herself, but he was very slim and agile. Later he told her that he was a squash enthusiast and that kept him up to scratch.

Time passed very quickly and Lee found she had enjoyed herself far more than she had expected to, for she had made herself believe that she would never enjoy anything again. They returned to the Lawleys' home in Mel's car, for Brett had left his behind; it would have been stupid to travel in two cars. Brett invited himself in for a coffee and Sandra said, 'You can stay overnight if you like,' but he refused to put them out. He left about one o'clock in the morning, thanking them for a lovely evening.

Lee didn't know whether she was pleased or not that Brett had just left casually without even expressing the hope that he might meet her again sometime. She had told herself all the evening that she hoped he wouldn't ask for a date because she had made up her mind that she would never get involved with a man again. She was afraid that

Des might take his revenge again when he was free.

It wouldn't be fair to any man to put him in that danger and she felt that if Des could kill in cold blood as he'd done, not on the spur of the moment, but with premeditation, he could do it again, so it was up to her to see that no one else's life would be taken. But she hadn't been put in the position of having to refuse a date because she hadn't been asked for one and couldn't help feeling just a little bit peeved. She had liked Brett.

The following morning she sat talking over the breakfast table with Mel and Sandra and Mel's mother who had been in bed when they got back last night. 'Did you enjoy yourself, Lee?' asked Mrs. Lawley.

'Very much, thank you,' she replied.

'You must get out and stop brooding over what's happened in the past,' Mel told her.

'Brett's nice, isn't he?' remarked Sandra.

'Yes, very. Rather reserved I thought, until we started to dance.'

'Yes,' said Mel. 'It did him good to get out too. He's been brooding over something that happened in the past too. He married a girl when he was quite young, I don't think he was above twenty was he mother?'

'No, and Fiona was eighteen. They were both too young, particularly Fiona.'

'She led him a terrible dance,' said Mel. 'She shouldn't have got married at all for she was too fond of the opposite sex, loved to have a lot of admirers. He put up with a great deal from her and finally she left him.'

'And she claimed her share of the marital wealth, of course,' said Mrs. Lawley. 'That meant that he had to give her half of all he possessed though she had never contributed anything. He had to sell their home and the contents and share it with her. She claimed a substantial sum of money and was successful. She did very well

44

out of poor old Brett.'

'It made him very bitter,' said Sandra. 'He'd worked so hard for all they'd got. Since then he's been very successful in his work. He has a very important job.'

'And he's sworn never to trust a woman again,' said Mel.

'You can't blame him,' said Lee, feeling sorry for Brett. She didn't know how anyone could have done that to him, and it seemed to her that those who were not in fault often had to pay. It also made her feel better over the fact that he hadn't expressed a wish to see her again. She had believed it was because he hadn't taken to her, that there was something wrong with her, but it was because he wasn't interested in any woman.

The week-end break staying with Mel and Sandra did her good. The two older children called her auntie Lee and had obviously taken to her. Katie amazed her by reading something out of the Sunday newspaper to her and making comments like an adult. She saw that Mel and Sandra were quite amused over her surprise. 'She's been reading the papers for some time,' said Mel. 'I try to stop her because there are some things unsuitable for a child, but it's almost impossible, and she doesn't understand why there are some things she shouldn't read.'

Although she was so grown up in many ways she was very childlike in others having tantrums when she couldn't get her own way, and very jealous of her young brother. She would play with him and talk to him a lot as if she were years older than he was, but when her parents made a fuss of him she made it quite clear that she didn't like it. She wanted all their attention.

'I hope she grows out of that stupid jealousy,' said Mel, and then caught Lee's eyes almost apologetically, knowing that he had reminded her of what jealousy can lead to.

'You expect to see jealousy in a little child,' she said, 'but not in an adult.'

'You must remember, Katie,' said her mother, 'that we have had you much longer than we've had Paul so you've had more love from us than he has. You mustn't be selfish in not letting him have some of our attention the same as you do.'

'I know but . . . ' began Katie, and her father chimed in. 'No arguments, Kate,' he said, sternly. 'You're older than Paul and old enough to understand that Mums and Dads love all their children exactly the same. That's only fair.'

The fact that he had reminded her that she was old enough to understand seemed to sink in. Katie loved to think that she was grown up and her father's words took effect. Lee hoped they would have a lasting effect, but was sure they had no need to worry over their little one. There were only an exceptional few who let jealousy possess them as Des had done when he was long past his childhood days.

Brett had not told her he would like

to see her again, but Sandra said she would. 'It's been lovely having you stay with us,' she told her. 'You will come and stay with us again, won't you?'

'I would love to,' said Lee. 'Thanks for inviting me. I've had a lovely time, and I'd love to come and see the children again.'

'Well that's a promise, don't forget.'

'I won't,' said Lee, and meant it.

But once she was back home she slipped into her withdrawn attitude again. She went to work and worked hard. The evenings were spent at home, reading, watching television, doing a bit of sewing, and she felt her life was aimless.

She had enjoyed her week-end and the dinner dance, but without Mel to bully her into going out for entertainment she went without. She could have gone out with Jean, though Jean was becoming quite serious with Dave and was hardly likely to suggest making up a foursome again in view of what had happened the last time, though she had never for one moment blamed Lee for the tragedy.

Lee often found herself thinking about Brett and wondering if he was still bitter about the way his marriage had turned out. It would be a shame if he remained bitter for the rest of his life because she liked him very much and thought he ought to find happiness, yet she couldn't blame him for not wanting to trust another woman.

As far as she herself was concerned she felt she had no alternative other than to keep herself to herself. She couldn't plan a future because always at the back of her mind was the thought that Des would not be locked away for ever. One day he would be free. Free to harm her, and something told her he would as soon as he got the chance. Not only would he be hating her for finishing with him, but he would be hating her even more because he had had to serve a prison sentence for killing the person she had preferred to be with.

Occasionally she accepted invitations from Mel to go and see Sandra and the children. She had to have some interests and was perfectly safe in visiting her boss and his family, for he had been Des's boss too, and he respected him. And she knew she was always welcome there. Sometimes she would baby-sit for them when they were stuck for a baby-sitter, although Mel hated to make use of her like that. He wanted to see her having a good time.

'You've had time to get over that shock you had,' he kept telling her.

'I don't think I'll ever get over it,' she answered.

'If that young fellow who died could talk to you he would tell you, as I am doing Lee, that it's not fair that your life should be empty because of something that wasn't your fault.'

'I'm sure of that,' she said, for Roy had been such a nice young man. She didn't tell Mel her real worry. The worry that nagged at her all the time. If she told him she was worried over what would happen when Des was released he'd tell her she was silly. He would tell her that Des would have learnt his lesson by now and wouldn't risk losing his freedom again, but she wasn't so sure. She had seen the look on Des's face when he had been sentenced.

There was one occasion when Lee had been baby-sitting for Sandra and Mel when Brett called in to see Mel about something. Lee was just about to start on the delicious supper Sandra had left for her when he came.

'Would you like me to give Mel a message for you?' she asked, surprised at the pleasure she felt in seeing him again.

'No, thanks, I suppose it can wait.'

He was looking at the tempting food set before her and she said, 'Are you hungry? There's far too much for me here you know.'

'No, it's all right,' he smiled. 'I was just thinking how nice it all looked.'

'And I'll get fat if I eat it all myself,'

she laughed. 'I'll get a plate for you, and the coffee is almost ready.'

'If you insist, then I will,' he smiled.

She gave him the largest portion and he protested, but seeing that she didn't intend to take any back he started to eat and seemed to enjoy sitting there with her sharing the food.

'Do you often baby-sit for Mel and Sandra?' he asked.

'Only occasionally. Mel doesn't like to ask me, but I don't mind. They're good to me and they simply couldn't get anyone tonight and Mel had to meet some important business people. They're combining business with pleasure.'

'I'll get him to let me know the next time you're baby-sitting,' he grinned, 'so that I can come and share your supper again. This is delicious.'

He stayed and helped her to wash up afterwards and then sat chatting to her until Mel and Sandra returned. They were pleased to see him and to know that he'd kept Lee company.

While Mel and Brett discussed the subject Brett had come round to discuss, Sandra began to tell Lee about their evening out, all the people they'd met, and what they'd had to eat, and how much wine she'd drunk.

'Sounds as if you've had a lovely evening,' said Lee, thinking that it couldn't have been any more enjoyable than the one she'd had in Brett's company.

When Mel said he was ready to run Lee home Brett said, 'There's no need for you to go out again, Mel. I can drop Lee off.'

She gathered her things together and found herself sitting in his Mercedes. It glided along and in no time they arrived at her home.

'Thanks for a very pleasant evening,' he said.

'Thank you for keeping me company and also for running me home.'

They didn't seem to have anything else to say to each other so she wished him 'goodnight' and that was that.

He couldn't have disliked her company or he wouldn't have spent so much time with her this evening, but he didn't say anything about seeing her again. It was just 'goodnight', and he waited until she was nearly at the front door with her key in her hand before he drove away.

Of course she didn't really expect him to make a date with her after only seeing her twice, but he didn't even say, 'Be seeing you sometime,' just out of politeness, as people do, so she obviously made very little impact upon him.

'Well, I don't mind,' she told herself. But there had been a time when she was never without friends and she wished she could go back to those days for her life seemed so terribly empty now. It was her own fault, she knew, but she longed for the years to fly by. She wanted Des to be free in order to discover how he intended to behave. She wanted to know whether he would leave her alone to live her life as she wished.

If he had a remission for good conduct he would only serve three years in jail and half of that had gone now because the time he had been held in custody had been taken into account.

In eighteen months' time Lee would be just over twenty-three. Not too old to start making new friends, that was if Des left her alone to do so.

3

Lee only saw Brett intermittently over the next months and yet he was often on her mind. She thought of him being lonely like herself, for she still didn't go out very often, not being able to rid herself of the idea that she had to wait until Des was free before she could make plans for her future.

She never told of her fears to anyone, not even her parents, but just stored them up within her. Des still wrote to her although she had never replied to one of his letters. Her father had told her to ignore them completely and that is what she did. 'He'll soon grow tired of writing when he gets no reply, and it will let him see that you have no time for him at all,' said Mr. Foster.

She came from a happy family, having two married brothers, Keith and Steve, each having a young son and

daughter so there was always somewhere she could go visiting and that
was one way in which she spent some of
her leisure time.

She became an expert knitter and
dressmaker and was called upon to
make garments for every member of the
family. Her mother took full advantage
of her talents in this respect, but her
father got very annoyed when he saw
her busy every evening with knitting
needles or at the sewing-machine.

'That's no life for a young girl like
you,' he would say. 'You make yourself
useful like that and you'll never have a
bit of peace. You'll be at everybody's
beck and call. I saw my mother working
for hours on end on a sewing-machine
for other people. They took advantage
of her and she let them. I don't want to
see that happen to you.'

But Lee didn't mind if she was taken
advantage of. It filled in her leisure
hours having something to do for
someone.

Mel, like her father, was always

telling her off too because she was growing as quiet as a little mouse, neglecting to mix with people of her own age, and Lee was well aware that people had no patience with her.

Mel would do a good turn for anyone and when he discovered that one of his employees, Tom Forester, had a little son with a rare disease and that it had been suggested that he went to America for treatment, he suggested to the staff that they had a sponsored walk in order to raise sufficient money for young Timothy to go.

They arranged to walk ten miles to Moreton Lea, camp out for the night and walk the ten miles back home again on the Sunday, and of course Lee agreed to go on the walk with them.

These walks would continue until the necessary amount required for treatment in an American hospital had been raised. Members of Lee's family sponsored her for fifty pence a mile and friends sponsored her too so at ten pounds from each of them she would raise a good amount for the fund. If others could do as well as that they would soon be able to send the child on his way.

All the walkers assembled on the Saturday morning outside the works with the photographers from the local newspapers to take pictures and give them lots of publicity. Several business people in the town were donating to the fund and it was nice to know that publicity was being given to a good cause.

Lee was delighted to see Brett amongst the walkers and especially when he sought her out and came alongside her. He took a look at her training shoes and said, 'Hello, are you all set?'

'I am,' she smiled. 'I didn't know you'd be taking part.'

'Well, I knew you were,' he replied. 'Mel told me. I said I'd accompany him as Sandra can't make it with the young children.'

So he hadn't come just because he

knew she was on the walk, she told herself, but it was nice to know he would be with them until tomorrow.

They all set off in good spirits cheered on by local inhabitants. Lee found herself being in the charge of Mel and Brett. She didn't push herself on to them, they just took control of her and she couldn't say she wasn't pleased about it.

They walked through the town and on to the outskirts and were soon walking along winding narrow lanes having to keep a sharp look-out for motorists.

They planned to walk the first five miles and then take a break for something to eat. The pace was not too swift so that those less agile could keep up with the crowd.

Mel left Brett and Lee at times in order to join other walkers and encourage them on their way. He was the organiser of the march and wanted to see that everyone was okay.

Before they'd completed the first five

miles Lee, like several others began to feel a little soreness. 'I think I've got a blister coming on my heel, blast it,' she said. The country miles seemed very long ones to her. She wasn't usually one to moan but she was anxious in case she wouldn't be able to continue if the soreness got worse.

'Shows you're not used to walking,' said Brett. 'Do you think you ought to attend to it right away? It's stupid to let it really get bad before doing anything about it.'

'What can I do? I haven't any plasters with me. I never thought about getting a blister.'

'Mel's got some,' he said. 'He'd have to come well prepared,' and he went off to tell Mel they'd have to stop for a bit.

It appeared that there were others developing blisters too and so a halt was called while they attended to them. Lee was wearing a jumper and jeans and short socks with her training shoes so didn't have to bother taking off tights in order to examine her foot. She

61

believed it was the thickness of the socks that had caused her foot to get sore, but had put them on thinking they would be a protection. There was a large red patch on the back of her heel but it had not gone into a blister.

'That's a good thing,' said Brett, offering to fix the plaster for her. 'Better to protect it before the skin breaks.'

He examined her foot thoroughly. 'A nice shape,' he remarked, giving her a grin.

She wriggled her foot free. 'I'm ticklish. I can't let anyone hold my foot.'

He was having no trouble with his own feet and soon they were all on their way again. 'At least you've got the sense to wear the correct shoes,' he said, for many of the walkers were wearing shoes not suitable for a sponsored walk.

'Ten miles a day didn't seem all that far to walk,' said Lee.

'It isn't all that far except for those not used to walking.'

The weather kept fine and when they

had a break for lunch they found a nice grassy slope in a field where they could sit and enjoy the scenery and rest their weary feet.

Mel and Brett sat a little apart from the others. Sandra had packed some food for Brett as well as Mel and they swopped some of theirs for some of Lee's finding they had a terrific appetite after their long walk. They had a bottle of table wine which Lee enjoyed more than a cup of tea or coffee from a flask.

As they were chatting Des Palmer came up in the conversation. 'How much longer has he got to do before he's finished his time?' asked Mel.

'Less than a year,' she said. She always felt embarrassed when Des's name was mentioned, hating to feel she had had connections with a man of his character. Brett obviously knew all about him for he expressed no surprise when they discussed a man in prison.

'I've been thinking about when he comes out,' said Mel. 'He was good at his job and it would be awful to deprive him of the means of earning a living after he's served his sentence, but I'm not altogether keen to have him back on the staff.'

'Because of me?' asked Lee. 'I can leave to save any embarrassment.'

'I wouldn't hear of it,' he retorted. 'We'll wait and see if he asks for his job back. I don't believe that a person should go on being penalised once he's paid his debt, but you don't know whether people will want to work with a man who can draw a knife and ruthlessly kill someone.'

'Are you anxious to see him free?' Brett asked Lee.

'In a way I am,' she said. 'In another way I'm afraid. He writes to me but I don't reply. In fact I don't read his letters. I destroy them right away. But I am afraid he might not have given up the obssession that I belong to him and that no one else shall have me. He told me that, you know, but I didn't believe it and look what happened. I want him to be free so that I shall know what my fate will be, and yet I'm afraid. I only feel safe while he's locked up.'

Mel looked angry. 'Is that the way your thoughts have been running all the time he's been in jail? No wonder you haven't been going out and about. You're afraid? That's the reason?'

'Yes. And I don't want to bring any more trouble to anyone.'

'You think he'd do the same again?' asked Brett.

'I do.'

'I presume you've broken off the engagement by now?'

'Oh, yes. I broke it off before going out on that Sunday with Jean and her friends.'

'I don't believe it mentioned that in the papers,' said Brett. 'You were referred to as his fiancée.'

'But I wasn't. I wouldn't have gone out with another man if I'd still been engaged to Des. Did you think I was still engaged to him, Mel?'

'No. I don't know whether I learned from members of the staff that you had broken off the engagement, but I know you finished with him and that he had no right to interfere in your affairs.'

Lee remembered that Brett's wife had had numerous affairs with other men before leaving him and he may have been thinking she was like that so she said, 'I didn't go out of my way to make Des jealous. I gave him up because he hated me to look at anyone else and made my life a misery. He was even jealous of my love for my own family, and my girl friends. He wanted us to live a long way out of town away from everyone I knew so that there would be no one interfering in our married life, he said. He wanted to possess me body and soul and I was afraid to show any interest in anyone else at all.

'What he did was terribly wicked. I often think of Roy and his family. It was horrible. I could never forgive Des. I suppose I didn't say much because whatever I said I couldn't alter the fact that a nice young man had lost his life because of Des, and me, to a certain extent, because Des warned me that if he couldn't have me no one else would. But of course you don't take things like that seriously. I never dreamt he could be so wicked. I had only met Roy that day. I hardly knew him except that he was a happy-go-lucky, fine young man, and I'll never forget him.

'Jean, my friend, fixed an outing. We went fishing by the river with Dave and Roy and they had booked a meal for us at the Fieldhouse. I told Des where we were going, quite innocently, because he was trying to get round me to go to his place again. He said his mother had invited me to dinner that Sunday and I explained why I couldn't.'

After that little conversation Lee felt that Brett changed towards her, was more friendly, although she couldn't have complained that he hadn't been friendly before, but he hadn't seemed to want to draw closer to her. Perhaps he had thought she was a girl who made her young man jealous just as his wife must have made *him* jealous. The difference was that Brett hadn't gone and stabbed any of the men his wife had associated with.

As they continued on their way he asked several times if Lee's feet were okay. 'No more blisters coming?' he asked.

'No. I think my feet are getting used to the exercise now,' she smiled.

He offered to carry her knapsack for her but as he had his own to carry she refused so he went to help an elderly lady with hers. The poor woman was beginning to look hot and weary but was determined to finish the walk with the rest of them. They had slackened their pace a lot for the sake of those who were not so young.

As Mel had arranged for the camping equipment to be taken on in a van earlier in the day, no one was carrying anything more than personal belongings.

At last they arrived at Moreton Lea and the farm where they were being allowed to camp. The farmer's family was willing to help them pitch tents and prepare food for them so that before long they were eating barbecued sausages, chicken portions, chops and so forth until everyone had eaten their fill. Cups of tea or coffee were to be had at the farmhouse where the farmer's daughters were busy making beverages and people queued at the kitchen door where there was lots of laughter and chatter. The farmer was charging for the drinks and the profits were to go to their fund.

There were a couple of large tents which accommodated quite a number of people and they were separated into male and female quarters with much joking and larking about as they decided who slept with who. Lee was to share a large tent with about eight other females.

Before settling down for the night they sat around chatting and breaking into community singing. They were like one big happy family with a wonderful atmosphere between them. Lee found herself sitting by Mel and Brett and as the evening wore on Brett's arm stole around her waist giving her quite a thrill.

She couldn't help feeling that their little talk about Des had made him see her in a different light. He must have made up his own mind about her character for she was sure that Mel and Sandra would not have encouraged him to think badly of her. Now he was behaving as if he really liked her and Lee was feeling very happy in consequence.

Mel spent a lot of time seeing that all the walkers were okay. He was concerned over some of the older members, afraid that they might have taken on more than they were capable of. He felt they were his responsibility and was anxious to see that they had had enough to eat and were happy about their sleeping arrangements. That left Brett and Lee with long stretches of time on their own, and maybe Mel had thought of that too.

It was surprising the number of people who were putting plasters on their feet and it made Lee giggle. 'We do look a fright, some of us,' she said, looking at the plaster on her own foot. 'I'm afraid most of us have got out of the habit of walking and our feet are protesting at the strain that has been put upon them.'

'Are yours aching?' asked Brett.

'No. My heel was just a bit tender but it's been okay since you put the plaster on for me.'

There were spots of rain before they settled down for the night and they all expressed the hope that the tents were water-proof, and they needed to be as the night wore on for the rain started to fall in torrents and then for good measure came thunder and lightning.

The women began to cry out in fright. It certainly was an experience being in the middle of a field in a tent during a heavy thunderstorm. Lee hadn't realised how much more scaring it could be when camping. The noise of the thunder is muted a bit when one is in a brick building, but the canvas did nothing to soften the crashes which came right over their heads.

The women screamed, some of them in exaggerated fright so that before long the men were in with the women, perhaps some of them were a little afraid too and felt there was safety in numbers. They all huddled together waiting for the storm to pass, and there was plenty of giggling going on because the men were in the tents of the women.

Brett and Mel had come to join the women and it was surprising how much comfort Lee got from the thought that they were close at hand. The tents held out against the rain for a long time, but as the rain continued to belt down there were leaks here and there and bedding had to be moved to try and escape the incoming rain.

'I've never been camping before,' said Lee to Mel, 'and I don't think I'll ever be camping again after tonight.'

He laughed. 'It's all experience. Something to talk about in the future. Think how much it will add to the interest when you discuss this walk and mention the terrible storm in the night.'

After a time the farmer came along with his son, both of them carrying lamps. The fields were flooding and he told them he'd rung through to the police and they were arranging for them all to be moved over to the parish hall.

Transport was put on and there was no opposition at all to the proposition that they should be taken to the hall. They were greeted by welfare people who had been called in specially to attend to them. They took in the bedraggled lot and soon there were cups of hot drinks for them.

'It was such a lovely day,' were the comments, 'who'd have thought it would turn out like this,' and so on.

'We shall have earned the money for the fund,' said a good many as they began to spread out their sleeping bags and tried to settle off to sleep. The storm was gradually diminishing and the thunder was grumbling discontentedly in the distance by this time. No one cared where they slept now so long as they could get some sleep before morning and Lee didn't mind at all when she saw that Brett was bedding down beside her on the wooden floor.

'Are you okay?' he asked, and she told him she was fine.

She didn't expect to get any sleep lying in a sleeping bag on a wooden floor but the day out in the fresh air had made everyone tired and at last peace reigned except from the snores from those sleeping on their backs with their mouths wide open. Lee thought those snores would keep her awake but they didn't. She slept for hours and woke to find Brett watching her with a smile on his face. He didn't smile a lot and she thought how much younger and more boyish he looked when he did.

'Couldn't you sleep?' she murmured, still half asleep.

'Yes, I slept fine. I woke a few minutes ago.'

'Have you been watching me asleep? Did I snore or twitch, or anything?'

He laughed. 'You were perfectly still. I could hardly tell whether you were breathing or not.'

One or two were already up and those indefatigable community workers were there again making tea and coffee. People like this always seem to appear miraculously in times of crisis.

The sun was shining beautifully and when they were dressed and peeped outside it was amazing to find that most of the rain had dried up. There were muddy streaks on the streets proving that the force of the water had brought top soil from the fields with it, but apart from that no one would have dreamt they'd had such a night.

Mel was up and organising the return to their tents and preparations for cooking breakfast. Brett left Lee to go and give him a hand.

The grass was wet and soggy and they were glad to get breakfast over and start on their return journey. The second day was not going to be so easy as the first for yesterday they had set off fresh with no sore feet to begin with, but now there were many with throbbing corns and tender feet. Lee was glad that the sore spot on her heel had not developed into anything more painful.

Stops were numerous and on the last lap of the journey many of the walkers were obviously in discomfort making Lee feel that she would always give more thought to those who went on sponsored walks in the future. But a marvellous comradeship had developed amongst them all and they all expressed their willingness to take part in other walks until sufficient money had been raised to send the little boy to America for treatment.

'Shall you take part in the next one, Brett?' asked Lee.

'There's no reason why I shouldn't,'

he said. 'It hasn't been to bad has it? Shall you?'

'I expect so. Let's hope we don't have a terrific thunderstorm next time.'

Before the crowds broke up Mel invited Brett and Lee home. 'Sandra promised to have a nice meal awaiting us,' he told them.

'I feel scruffy,' said Lee.

'You look all right,' Mel said. 'No worse than the rest of us.'

'And at least you've got some colour in your cheeks for a change,' said Brett.

Mel had left his car at the works to be picked up when they returned and it was marvellous to get in and sit in comfort on the way to his home.

Sandra greeted them with a smile of sympathy. 'Are you all waiting to soak your poor feet?' she asked.

But they assured her they weren't so bad, unlike a good many of the walkers who would suffer from sore feet for several days to come.

'Makes you realise how lucky you are if you've got good feet when you meet some of those who haven't,' grinned Mel.

'What about the thunderstorm?' said Sandra. 'It scared me to death and I was indoors.'

They laughed at the recollections of the panic and Brett said, 'It gave the men a good excuse for being in the tents with the ladies.'

Sandra had a lovely meal of roast pork with apple sauce, baked potatoes and stuffing, with plenty of vegetables, and Lee told her she loved the crackling off pork. The children were in bed, although Katie was awake and reading, 'So we can have our meal in peace,' Sandra told them.

When Lee knew that Katie was awake she asked if she could go up to her first and say 'Hello', and the little girl was delighted to see her. She had her bed crowded with all the fluffy toys she possessed and said she was reading them a fairy tale. She had long passed the stage when she required her mother to read to her.

She had a charming bedroom with wall paper covered with tiny rosebuds. Her curtains and duvet cover matched perfectly and Katie looked very pretty lying there in such comfort. Lee saw that Brett had followed her too to see Katie and she felt there was quite a wistful look in his eyes as he looked down on the little child. If his own marriage had turned out all right he would have had little ones of his own by now.

Lee gave Katie a kiss and wished her goodnight and then left Brett to have a few words with her.

'She doesn't look at all sleepy,' she said to Sandra when she got down again.

'No, she's always like that, but she goes out like a light. She'll be wide awake one moment and the next she's fast alseep so I just leave her. She's no trouble.'

'Do you think you've got a genius there?'

'Yes, if she takes after me,' said

Sandra, laughing.

'After me, you mean,' said Mel. 'I'm the brains of the family.'

Lee laughed at their friendly banter and thought they didn't know how lucky they were to be so happily married with a lovely young family.

After the delicious meal they sat talking until well past midnight. Brett had promised to run Lee home again as he'd done before so she didn't have to worry about transport.

She almost fell asleep in his car on the way home and when they arrived at her home he said, 'Wake up, sleeping beauty.'

She gave a huge yawn. 'Oh, Brett, I'm so tired I don't think I'll have the energy to undress myself.'

'Want me to come and help you?' he laughed.

'Better not,' she said. 'I'd start giggling and wake up my Mum and Dad.'

'Another time,' he laughed, and she wished him goodnight and thanked him for the lift. He helped her with all her paraphernalia, waiting until she had unlocked the door and pushed every-thing inside before leaving her. As he walked back to the car he said, 'See you on the next sponsored walk.'

'Oh, yes,' she answered, and tired as she was she couldn't help thinking that was the first time he had ever mentioned anything about seeing her again on leaving her, and that was only to refer to the next sponsored walk.

He didn't intend to get involved with her, that was obvious, but she couldn't say she blamed him. It was safer for him not to.

She left all her gear in the hall to be removed in the morning when she was more lively and went off to bed feeling she'd had a lovely week-end although her feet were feeling tender, and in spite of the storm which had almost washed them and their tents away. As Mel said, it was all experience, something to talk about.

It would be nice if she had someone

special to talk to, she thought, as she crept into bed shortly afterwards to fall into a deep sleep. Her last thoughts were that she could sleep for a week. She often lay awake for hours unable to sleep. She would think about Des Palmer locked up with so many other prisoners. It was a hateful thought, but how could they deal with people who did wicked things? People knew the penalty for wrong doing, but it obviously didn't stop some of them from spoiling their own lives as well as those of other people.

4

The sponsored walk together with the donations given by many business people raised sufficient money to send young Timothy Forester to America with his parents to receive expert attention and everyone was delighted. In the event of a cure being possible the organisers of the walk, headed by Mel, promised that other walks would be arranged to provide any more money that might be needed.

For the time being everything was in abeyance until they knew how things would go so Lee, who had looked forward to seeing Brett on another walk, knew that she would have to wait for some time. Perhaps it was as well because she was getting to like him a lot, found herself thinking about him all the time, although she had made up her mind she wouldn't get involved with another man. She knew she would walk another twenty miles or more, suffer another terrifying thunderstorm just to be with him again.

But she didn't have to suffer any of those things in order to see him for he rang through to the works one day and asked Mel if he could talk to Lee. Mel lost no time in bringing her to the phone and left her alone in his office to talk to him.

'One of your admirers wants to speak to you,' he had teased her, with a grin.

She was thrilled to hear Brett's voice though she tried not to sound too eager in accepting his invitation to go out for a meal with him on Saturday evening.

'Mel tells me there won't be another walk for the time being so I thought, 'Why wait for a walk.' Would you like to go out?'

'Yes, thanks. I thought we'd be tramping the roads again. We did wonderfully well, didn't we? I hope the little boy finds someone to cure him after all that effort.' She knew she was talking for talking's sake, feeling rather nervous.

'Yes, I hope he gets completely well again. Well, what about Saturday evening? You'll be free?'

'Yes. What time?'

'I'll call for you around seven thirty, okay?'

'Fine. I'll look forward to that.'

'So will I.'

When Mel came back into his office she turned to him, her eyes alight. 'Brett wants me to go out with him on Saturday night.'

'Good,' he smiled. 'It's time you both got yourselves out of the blues.'

Lee was ready to go out and enjoy herself again. She wasn't nursing a broken heart over anyone and there was no reason why she shouldn't be happy, she supposed, but she knew that Brett had been grieving over his wife's infidelity and was bitter about her greediness in getting as much as she could out of him after the break-up of their marriage. Lee didn't know how a woman could do that to a man who had done no wrong to her. Brett was bound to be cautious as far as women were concerned in the future.

She found joy in going shopping for a new outfit and that pleased her parents. They had been longing for her to get over all that business of Des and to start living again.

Just because she'd accepted an invitation to go out for a meal with Brett didn't mean that she was going to get involved seriously with him, Lee told herself.

But for all that she was excited when he called for her. She had bought a smart dress with floral skirt and blouse type top in Broderie Anglaise and looked really lovely in it. Her dark hair was shining and contrasted well with the white of her dress. She didn't wear a lot of make up. Just enough to enhance her best points, like outlining her perfect mouth with a not too bright lipstick, and making her eyes even more appealing with the addition of eye shadow.

When Brett called for her she was looking very much different from last week when she had been dressed for walking and spending the night camping, and the expression in his eyes made her aware of the fact that he found her much more attractive now than he did then.

He took her to a smart place where there was a cabaret following the meal. They were both feeling a little reserved in each other's company on this their first date, completely alone. She thought about the times when she had been out with Des Palmer, and wondered if Brett was thinking about the times he had brought his wife out like this.

'What are you thinking about?' he asked. 'You seem miles away.'

'Thinking about how long it's been since I came out like this,' she said, telling him only half the truth. 'I haven't been going out a lot since, well, you know.'

'I know, though I can't understand why you shouldn't go out and enjoy yourself. You said you don't care for that fellow any more.'

'Everyone seems to think I ought to be able to go on living normally in spite of what happened, they don't understand that it was a traumatic experience for me. I can't just dismiss it from my mind.'

'It's been a long time ago now. You can't alter anything by dwelling on it all the time.'

'But I can't help feeling guilty for a young man's death.'

'You mustn't feel like that,' he said, looking appalled. 'You weren't to blame in any way.'

'Some would blame me. I should have taken more notice of Des's warning.'

'You couldn't have known he meant it seriously. Lots of things are said when people are quarrelling.'

'He meant what he said, that no one else should have me. Suppose he still means it?'

'At the moment he can't get at you or anyone else, can he?'

'No. I don't desire him to be locked away for ever, but can people have any peace when a person like that is set free? It won't be long now before he's free and I'm dreading it. I don't know what he will do.'

'Don't think about it, Lee,' Brett said. 'Enjoy yourself.'

'It's easier said than done. But I will tonight,' she smiled. 'I'm sorry to keep harping on the subject, but it's always there in my mind.'

'You feel free to talk to me about it,' he said. 'You don't want to keep it all bottled up inside and be afraid to express your fears. I can understand how you feel, though I'm afraid I've never given such matters much thought before.'

'Neither did I. But there must be lots of people living in fear when someone who has attacked them or someone else is free again.'

'Mel worries over you, you know. He often talks about you. He and Sandra think a lot of you.'

'They've been very good to me. Des worked for him and he could have blamed me for all the trouble because Des was a quiet sort of man at work, creating no trouble there, but Mel has never made me feel to blame. Is that why you asked me out tonight? Did Mel make you feel sorry for me?'

'No, I did not ask you out for that reason,' he retorted. 'I asked you out because I wanted to see you again. I haven't been in the mood, either, for mixing with people . . . girls, anyway, but I know you're not like Fiona. Not in the least.'

It was nice of him to tell her that and she decided to enjoy herself. 'We are only young once,' she thought.

And once Lee had decided not to worry any more she became more like her normal self, full of life and fun. In no time she and Brett became special friends. He told her she seemed like a different person from the one he had first met when they were with Mel and Sandra. 'Then you seemed quiet and stand-offish,' he told her. 'Mel wanted us to be friends because he was concerned over you, but you gave me little encouragement.'

Lee could have told him that he himself didn't invite her to give him any encouragement at first. Now they were getting to know each other as they really were, having cast off their miseries.

They began to see each other nearly every evening, mixing with his friends and her own now that it was known that she was in circulation again. He found her a gay and exciting companion, and she was proud to be seen with Brett who could be good company too now that he chose to be.

He took her to meet his parents and she invited him home to meet hers. He met her brothers and their families and she met his brother, Phillip, twenty-four and five years younger than Brett, and there was his sister Angela twenty-two, a little younger than Lee.

Often when they went round to Brett's home they didn't bother to go out for they were a nice family group and enjoyed chatting together, listening to records and having plenty of laughs.

The more Lee got to know Brett the more easy-going she found him, an easy person to get along with and so she concluded the fact that his marriage had failed couldn't have been his fault. She was sure he was a very tolerant person and there were no signs of the jealousy she had encountered when she was with Des. Brett's brother often teased her and fooled around with her and that wouldn't have done for Des. He would have gone mad and accused her of encouraging his attention, thinking more of his brother than she did of him. It was lovely to be carefree and not afraid to show her affection for someone else without the fear of upsetting the man in her life.

The first time Brett kissed her outside her home in his car it had been a very brotherly type of kiss, nothing to carry her into the heights at all, but that was only the beginning. Now he kissed her goodnight far more passionately, and looked for opportunities to get her alone so that they could do more than kiss. After a time she began to feel disappointed if they didn't get a chance to be alone for a time to show their affection for each other.

Brett had been married and she wouldn't have been surprised if he had wanted to carry his love-making further than just being nice to her, holding her in his arms to kiss her and caress her, but he was very patient. He was not rushing into a second marriage without a lot of thought. In fact he hadn't mentioned anything about marriage, but Lee's thoughts had been in that direction quite soon after finding how much she cared for him.

She began to lie awake at night, not

thinking about Des now, and what he might do to her when he was free, but longing for Brett to propose to her. She was so afraid that he might not want to sample married life again, and if he was merely amusing himself with her she couldn't blame him for she had told him right from the start that she was afraid to become involved with someone else for fear of what Des might do. Brett might have decided to keep her company until Des was out of prison, for he had said that while he was locked away he couldn't do any harm, and he could drop her as soon as he felt he was in danger.

She couldn't make herself believe that Brett was like that. She was sure he wasn't just playing with her, amusing himself for the time being, but you could never be quite sure of anything. He told her she was lovely, that his life had changed since he'd met her, and paid her many compliments, but he hadn't said a word about being in love with her or wanting to marry her. And

94

when a girl reaches the age of twenty-three she is ready for marriage. In fact Lee would have been married to Des a long time ago if he hadn't acted so stupidly.

Brett's sister Angela had been bringing a young man home intermittently for a year or two. His name was Roger and as he was quite a good bit older than Angela her family considered him not at all suitable for her. Their criticism of him had influenced her a great deal, but now she had made up her mind that it didn't matter what anyone else thought about Roger. He was the man she wanted to marry and so they announced their engagement and their intention of getting married very soon.

'Roger has seen a lovely house for sale,' she told her family, 'and there's no reason why we should delay our wedding. It's near to Roger's works and I love the area where it is situated.'

Seeing that she had made up her mind and that nothing was going to make her change it her family decided to give their blessing to the wedding and their attitude towards Roger changed. He was welcomed into their fold and her parents began to look forward to the wedding of their only daughter, planning to give her a really nice wedding reception.

Lee could see in a way why the Lawleys had objected to Angela marrying Roger. He was well into his thirties. His dark hair was rapidly receding and he wore glasses with thick lenses because his eyesight was poor. Their daughter looked so young and girlish it seemed impossible that she could have chosen a man like Roger, yet when you got to know him he was very likeable. He was a quiet, very intelligent man, with a dry sense of humour. He and Angela were obviously mad about each other and couldn't wait to be married.

'Would you like to come and see the house we're going to buy?' Roger asked Brett and Lee.

'Yes, I'd like to,' said Brett. 'Would you Lee?'

'I would. I love looking round houses.' She had done plenty of that with Des just before giving him up and it had been exciting trying to find a house to suit them, but frustrating when Des turned down many lovely houses because he wanted to live further out of town.

Off they went in Roger's car. Whatever job he had, thought Lee, he was obviously not short of money for his car was an expensive model and when they arrived to see the house that was just as obviously an expensive model too. It stood in its own grounds, was a five-bedroomed type, with several bathrooms. A wide staircase ran up from the hall with a long landing along which windows on one side overlooked the gardens.

The house had not been lived in before it was absolutely new and Angela was quite prepared to accept any suggestions with regard to furniture and soft furnishings. Lee went round with her into each room and they would stand there trying to imagine what sort of furniture would be suitable here and there. Lee had become quite good on a sewing-machine and when Angela said she would be hopeless at making her own curtains she offered to assist her.

'I wouldn't offer to make curtains for your lounge, those will need to be tailored by experts, but I would help with bathroom curtains and the kitchen ones, even the bedrooms if you'd like.

'Well, it would save a lot of money. What do you think, Roger?'

'I leave that entirely to you girls to sort out,' he said.

'You can get curtains and wallpaper to match,' said Angela, 'that's what I'd like.'

The men stood listening to the girls discussing curtains and lampshades and Lee thought Roger might have been contented to leave all that side of the soft furnishing to Angela but he also had ideas on how he would like the place furnished and he and Angela seemed to agree on almost everything.

When they had finally left the house they were still discussing furniture and the décor for the rest of the evening. The four of them had decided to go for a meal to round off the evening and when they were eating the delicious food put before them Roger told Angela to take particular note of the dishes being served.

'You won't expect me to be able to cook this right away?' she smiled.

'I'll give you a few days to reach this standard,' he smirked.

She turned to Lee in mock dismay. 'Do you know anything about cooking, besides sewing?'

'Afraid I don't,' said Lee.

'You'll have to get cracking if you're thinking of getting married,' said Brett.

She looked at him and their eyes met, making her heartbeats quicken. Was marriage to her in his mind? They could hardly tear their eyes apart.

She quite enjoyed the next few weeks for Angela took advantage of her offer to help her with her curtains and they both worked together measuring up and cutting the material to the lengths required. Lee wouldn't have offered to make them up if she hadn't had quite a lot of experience over the past months. When she hadn't been going out she'd done lots of sewing which included making lined curtains for her mother and sisters-in-law. Most people would much prefer to pass on their sewing jobs to other people, as Lee had discovered.

And then she helped, with Angela's mother too, to get the house cleaned up in readiness for the carpet fitters to come in, and the furniture deliverers. All the kitchen units in the large kitchen needed to be washed before use, the windows had to be cleaned, though they would get a window cleaner eventually for the outside, but at the moment they had no one in mind so the men helped.

Gradually they saw the house becoming more like a home. Curtains were fixed, decorating was completed, and here Brett, his brother Phillip and even Angela's father had all given Roger a hand to make light work of it. They all enjoyed getting the place ready for the young couple.

By this time Angela's family had got to know Roger so well and liked him so much they wondered why they had ever thought him the wrong man for Angela.

Angela's mother had been to evening classes and was an expert at making lampshades and so she made some for the bedrooms in the same material as the curtains. The main bedroom was in deep blue and light blue shades on a white background and Angela had shopped around to get her valance and duvet to match perfectly. The carpet was in blue and the bedroom furniture in white, the wardrobes being fitted so that they'd only had to get the dressing-table which fitted all along one wall with a huge mirror in the centre.

Angela's family had bought that for their wedding present.

'You've made these curtains perfectly,' said Mrs. Lawley. 'You could be a professional, Lee.'

Lee flushed with pleasure at her praise and Brett laughed. 'She's getting her hand in mother,' he said, and again Lee wondered if that was a hint that he was going to propose to her.

If he came across her in a room on her own, contemplating some job or other that had to be done, before she knew where she was she would find herself in his arms and though she tried to treat it all very lightly her heart would start fluttering wildly at his touch and she would wish that they were alone. She often wondered if he felt the rapid heartbeats. There was always someone to pounce on them and cry, 'What's going on in here, I thought you were fixing that switch, Brett,' or, 'Angela says have you seen the scissors, Lee?'

Before the kitchen furniture arrived

they would sit down in the kitchen on packing cases, or anything available and drink coffee from mugs, talking until quite late, reluctant to leave the house when there were so many jobs to be done and the wedding drawing nearer.

Lee was always looking in Brett's direction. She would notice an unruly lock of hair falling on his forehead, would watch him talking, smiled when he smiled, which was more often than when she first met him. It seemed he was getting over his broken marriage for she would often hear him and Roger having a good laugh together over something probably not fit for girls to hear. He couldn't laugh like that if he was still bitter and broken-hearted.

She found joy in watching his hands as he was doing a job. Strong capable hands. Anything that belonged to him made her heart full of pleasure. She would see his car and because it was his it seemed to stand out for her against all others on the car park.

She became accustomed to seeing

him dressed in various ways. When he was doing jobs he would wear tatty old jeans and a T-shirt. Sometimes he would call for her in slacks and a jumper if they were not going anywhere particular, but when he took her out somewhere special he had an assortment of suits to fall back on. On those occasions he looked extremely handsome to her and she was thrilled to be with him.

He had only to take her hand when they were entering some place and her legs would feel all trembley. He was always reaching for her hand and it gave her such joy to realise that it gave him so much pleasure to hold her hand. He was forgetting his disastrous marriage and she was feeling less haunted by the face of a dying young man. That, she could never forget, but she was able to think about it now without so much distress.

She didn't lie awake at night thinking about Des in prison any more, either. He was paying for his own wickedness and had only himself to blame for any misery he was suffering.

She could put the past behind because she was in love. She loved Brett far more than she'd ever loved Des even before she'd known how stupidly jealous he could be. She was living just for Brett. Everything she could do to please him she did. She dressed to please him and when he complimented her on her appearance she was in the seventh heaven. A smile across a crowded room from him lifted her to the heights.

She was grateful to Mel for bringing them together and they often visited him and Sandra being greeted by the children with great whoops of joy and being bombarded with questions and having to see all their toys. Brett would find himself assembling a model aeroplane while Lee would be reading to Katie, or more likely Katie would be reading to her for she considered herself far too adult to be read to these days.

Mel and Sandra would be at the wedding of Angela and Roger, of course, and that took up most of the conversation these days and young Katie was thrilled because she was going to be a bridesmaid. 'I wonder what we'll talk about when the wedding's over,' said Lee, 'and what we'll do when there are no more jobs left to be done in their home.'

'Maybe we'll be planning for another wedding,' smiled Sandra, and Lee knew she was thinking of her and Brett. It would be absolutely wonderful if Brett asked her to marry him. Wishful thinking on her part, but wishes can come true.

5

Lee hadn't had a letter from Des for ages which was not surprising considering she had never answered one of his letters in the past most of which she had destroyed without even opening them. It had been a relief when he'd stopped writing and she was hoping that he had accepted the fact that there could never be anything between them again and that he would leave her alone when he was free.

It was a bit of a shock, therefore, to find a letter one morning in the post from him. She opened it as if expecting it to go off like a letter bomb in her hand but she had to know what he was writing about for he would be free very soon now.

If it had been from anyone but Des she might have been touched by the contents. He told her how prison life had affected him. His life was ruined; he would never get over these years he had spent locked away from everyone, particularly herself. She couldn't help thinking of the life he had taken. He never mentioned that, was only sorry for himself. He might feel he had been hard done by but nothing could alter the fact that he was a murderer. The life he had taken could never be given back and there was never a sign of remorse. Roy's family would never forgive him, she was sure.

He went on to say that the only thing that had kept him going was the thought that she might forgive him and take him back again after he'd paid his debt for what he'd done. His mother kept him informed of her activities. This annoyed her, and the fact that she hadn't been going out and about a lot had given him hope that she was waiting for him. That she realised now how much she loved him and that they belonged together.

If Des's mother had been keeping

him well informed it was a wonder she hadn't told him that Lee had been going out regularly with another man for the past few months. Lee had nothing against his parents. She liked his mother and was very sorry for her. She supposed it had been easy for her to keep a check on Lee's activities for they lived in the same town and knew people who lived close to Lee. In that case she would know that her son's old girl friend was no longer keeping herself in isolation at home while Des was in prison. Perhaps she had not mentioned this to Des to save him unhappiness while he was there. If the thought that she was waiting for him was the only thing that kept him going she couldn't really blame his mother for trying to keep up his spirits, but it was going to be something of a shock for Des when he was released to discover that she was no longer sitting at home like a recluse. For a time she had had no heart to go out enjoying herself after what had happened to Roy. Anyone who had had such an experience as that would take a long time to get over it, she was sure, and couldn't imagine how Des could believe that she would still want him when he had proved so ruthless.

His letter ended by telling her that if she would stand by him when he came out he would do anything in the world for her to make up for causing her so much unhappiness. 'I swear I'll make up to you,' he had written. 'I have realised how stupid I was since I've been here. I have hours and hours to think over the way I behaved and everything will be different, I promise.'

Lee knew that many girls had stood by their men no matter what they had done. That was because they loved them and could forgive, but Lee had stopped loving Des. It wasn't a matter of standing by him, forgiving him, or anything like that, she just simply didn't want him any more and it had been like that before he had committed that terrible crime. He had killed her love before she'd agreed to go out with Jean and Roy and Dave that Sunday. Now she refused to feel condemned for not standing by her man.

She wasn't so hard that she couldn't have some sympathy for him and his letter touched her although it was so full of self pity, but she wished he hadn't written to her. She didn't know whether she should continue to ignore him or write and tell him there was no point in him having any hope as far as she was concerned; yet he had to face the fact sooner or later that she didn't want him at any price. Nothing he could do would make her change her mind.

She thought of showing Brett the letter but Angela's wedding day was so near she decided to leave it until afterwards. It was a shame to involve Brett in her worry when he and all his family were so looking forward to the wedding.

Her parents worried about Des communicating with her again. 'I've always felt sympathy for some of these young people who get themselves into trouble and have been sentenced to long prison sentences,' said her father, 'and I've sometimes thought that the sentences were too severe, but now I understand how people who have been involved with them feel.'

'So do I,' said Mrs. Foster. 'How can they be sure they'll be safe when the prisoner is released? No doubt many of them learn from their mistakes and the term in prison puts them off doing anything else wrong, but for many who are anxious to make a fresh start, there must be others who have stored up bitterness and resentment in jail. They have not been reformed and can be even more dangerous when they get the chance.'

Lee determined to put Des out of her mind to concentrate on Angela's wedding. When the day arrived the weather couldn't have been nicer. It was a calm sunny day with scarcely a breeze to disturb her wedding veil, and no sign of a cloud in the sky.

Angela lived up to her name on this special day for she looked absolutely angelic. Lee couldn't help feeling it was a shame that Roger was losing his hair and looked so much older than his bride and couldn't help looking at Brett and thinking how proud she would be if it was her wedding day and he was her groom. But it wasn't very fair to judge people by their looks she knew, especially now she knew Roger and that he had a much better disposition than many a more handsome and younger man. He adored Angela and she him so that was what really counted. Lee had been carried away by Des's good looks in the beginning and look where that had got *her*.

Katie and the other little bridesmaids looked adorable too and were very excited. Lee was wearing a lovely pink two piece and a shiny black straw hat trimmed with pink roses. Brett had pinned a pink carnation to her lapel, and in her high-heeled black patent shoes she looked beautiful and almost as happy as the bride. There is always something radiant-looking about a bride and bridegroom. The happy smile on Roger's face made him look years younger than he was. Lee thought about Brett's wedding day for he must be looking back on those memories and his parents were bound to be thinking about it too. But Brett's thoughts today couldn't have been unhappy ones for he was laughing and joking with all the guests and thoroughly enjoying himself.

Lee sat with Brett at the table of the bride and groom and felt quite honoured. Everyone seemed to be taking it for granted that she was Brett's girl and she hoped very much that was how he was regarding her for they were spending almost all their leisure time together these days.

As a member of the bride's family he had to do his share of entertaining the guests, see that they were well supplied with drinks and that everyone was happy, not feeling ignored in any way, yet he managed to make Lee feel that she was top priority. Even when he was talking to someone else he made her feel she was still on his mind and came first.

'I suppose it wouldn't be fair to say you look as good as the bride,' he smiled, 'for our Angie looks stunning, doesn't she? But you must be the second best girl here today.'

'Flatterer,' she smiled, pleased at his remarks.

'Actually, you are the very best here today in my estimation,' he grinned. 'You look beautiful. Pity there are so many people about.'

'You look beautiful yourself,' she smiled, mischievously. He was certainly looking marvellous in an off white suit and his dark hair seemed to be gleaming. How could his wife have gone off with other men, and then left him altogether?

She had expected, when she first went out with him, to find there was something about him to give his wife cause to want to get away from him, but if there was, she hadn't discovered the cause herself.

Brett had hidden Roger's car so that no one could play tricks on them. Kippers in the engine and daubs all over the windows of the car are amusing to everyone except those who have to remove them. When it was time for Angela and Roger to set off on their honeymoon they left in Brett's car which caused lots of disappointment amongst the men because they had been deprived of their fun, but there were lots of cheers and laughter when, before the guests had had time to go back into the hotel, Roger and Angela reappeared in their own car which had been successfully hidden just round the corner and they'd swopped cars.

They drove slowly past waving to their guests and smirking all over their faces at their cleverness in escaping their tricks.

Brett stood with his arms round Lee's waist having a jolly good laugh with all the others.

As soon as the bride and groom were on their way many of the guests started to leave as is usually the case, and others were going round to the home of the bride's mother to finish off the celebrations there. Lee knew that Brett's mother had been very busy cooking and preparing food at home for those who ended up at their house after the reception.

Mrs. Lawley had been just a little tearful as she had watched her daughter driven away by Roger, but now she had too much to do looking after the remaining guests to indulge in tears. Sandra and Mel had been at the wedding, of course, and Lee had noticed the resemblance between Mel's father and Brett's for he and his wife had been amongst the guests.

Mr. Lawley had looked a little emotional too, Lee thought, as his eyes had rested on his beautiful daughter. It's not only women who feel tearful at weddings. Fathers too must feel a sense of loss when they see their sons and daughters starting off to make a new life for themselves independent of parents.

As soon as most of the guests had left Brett suggested to Lee that they went for a run out somewhere for it was still early. 'I could do with some fresh air, couldn't you?'

'I wouldn't mind a run out,' she said, so they wished the remaining relatives cheerio and off they went. It was a beautiful evening, the sun slowly sinking and the sky more beautiful than any painter could produce.

Brett knew how to find the best beauty spots and driving leisurely they soon found themselves travelling along winding narrow lanes, climbing steadily until they were at the summit of a hill and then he stopped the car so that they could sit and feast their eyes on the surrounding beauty. They looked across hills and valleys, watched the lambs playing in the field.

Lee stretched and ran her fingers through her hair. The black straw hat was lying on the back seat. 'It's been a glorious day,' she said. 'I wonder how Angela is feeling now.'

'Did you envy her today?'

'Of course. Most girls would envy a beautiful bride.'

'She was beautiful. We're a good-looking family,' he grinned.

'Conceited,' she murmured. 'Are you including yourself?'

'But of course,' he smiled, and then he pulled her towards him to give her a kiss.

'Would you marry a man who's been divorced?' he asked, suddenly very serious, and her heart began to race.

'Depends on who the man was. Whether it was his fault and all the circumstances.'

'Do you think I could have been to blame for my marriage break-up?'

'According to Mel you both married too early and Fiona wasn't the type to settle down to matrimonial bliss.'

'I tried to save the marriage, mainly because of Mum and Dad. I knew how upset they'd be. They're old fashioned and have no time for people who divorce and don't try to make their marriage a success. But Fiona wouldn't try to make a success of our marriage. She hated work of any kind. The house was always a mess so that I was too ashamed to take business colleagues home. I used to try to be loving but it made no difference, we were always quarrelling. She would go out to work when it suited her, but never kept a job more than a few weeks. And then she realised that if we separated she could claim half of all I had and the idea of having plenty of money appealed to her. I had to sell the house and give her half of what we had. That makes a man feel very bitter I can tell you.'

'It's enough to put a man off women for good.'

He was silent for a time, thinking about it, and went on again. 'We were often invited out to dine with important people, and she liked that all right, but when it came to entertaining them she didn't want to know. She would throw a fit if I dared to mention that I wanted to invite people home. Anyway I couldn't have relied on her to put on a decent spread. I offered to get someone in to help her but she resented all who came and they soon left.'

'You can't blame yourself for the marriage failing. You did your best.'

'I did blame myself. You feel you have failed somewhere along the line. I do believe that marriage vows should not be broken; there's no point in making them if you don't believe that, but they didn't mean anything to Fiona. She was very pretty and attracted men and that was what she liked, but I'm sure it was the thought of being able to claim so much money from me that made her want a divorce. She couldn't get enough money and I daresay she's spent all that she had from me by now.'

'I'll bet you vowed never to have anything else to do with girls.'

'I did,' he smiled. 'I was dreadfully miserable and disillusioned when I first met you. And you weren't on top of the world, either, were you?'

'No. I was still in a state of shock over what Des had done and I suppose in a way I was feeling I was responsible in the same way as you felt responsible for your broken marriage. But neither of us was really to blame for things going wrong.'

'You changed my life for me, Lee, gave me the will to make a fresh start. I began to feel, after I'd known you properly, that life could be exciting again. Marriage could be a fine thing with the right person. But could you marry a man who's been married and divorced?'

'If you are asking me if I could marry you, Brett, the answer is 'yes'.'

'Sure? I've almost forgotten my first marriage, I can quite easily put it right out of my mind altogether. I'd do everything I could to make our marriage a success and make you happy.'

They just sat looking at each other

and suddenly he caught her in his arms and just held her tight. 'We could be happy together, Lee,' he said.

She turned her face to kiss him and said, 'I'm sure we could. We *have* been happy together,' but then she remembered Des's letter and drew away from him.

'What is it?' he asked, anxiously.

'I had a letter from Des Palmer the other day.'

His eyes narrowed. 'You didn't tell me.'

'No. Well we were all so happy about Angie's wedding I decided to put it out of my mind until afterwards.'

'What's he got to say?'

'I'll let you read it. He hopes I'm going back to him when he comes out of prison and I'm afraid of how he might react when he knows I'm not.'

'You should have told me, love. You shouldn't worry over him on your own. Well, that settles it. We'll get married without delay and then he'll know there's nothing doing. You can write and tell him you have a husband to take care of you.'

'But wouldn't you be scared? He's a wicked man.'

'Well, if you are in any danger, Lee, I want to be near you. You need someone with you. You'd have a nervous breakdown worrying on your own.'

She clung to him and there were tears in her eyes. 'Oh, Brett, I love you, very much, but I couldn't bear it if anything happened to you through marrying me.'

'It won't,' he said, confidently. 'I should think he's had enough of jail; he wouldn't risk having to go back.'

He put his arm around her and then said, 'Drat this steering-wheel. Let's go for a walk, Lee.'

They got out of the car and walked by means of a public right of way across the fields and then coming upon a tree with a good wide trunk he leaned against it and pulled her towards him.

'We're going to get married, Lee,' he said, excitement in his voice.

'If you're not going to worry, I'm not. I'm terribly happy, Brett.'

His kisses now that he knew she was going to belong to him became much more passionate than any he had given her before and soon he had drawn her down on to the grassy slope so that they could lie in each other's arms. She had always thought that couples who made love in the open air like this were really brazen, but now she didn't care. She was happy in Brett's arms and didn't care who knew it.

'I'll get a special licence,' he said, in between kisses and petting.

'Do you want to get married that quickly?'

'I think we'd better, don't you?'

She giggled. 'It would be lovely.'

And it was so wonderful being made love to like this that she almost let him take her there and then but knew she mustn't.

Darkness began to fall but they were reluctant to return to the car.

'I can't believe you've accepted my

proposal,' he said. 'I've been planning all day to ask you. You looked so gorgeous and you watched our Angie with such a wistful look in your eyes I've been dying to tell you that you could be a bride as soon as you chose. I love you more than I've ever loved before. I thought I knew what love was all about when I got married but was soon disillusioned. Now I'm old enough to have more sense in choosing a suitable wife. I feel that my marriage to Fiona had to end because we weren't right for each other. But we're right for each other, Lee, aren't we?'

'I'm certain we are.'

'I haven't rushed you, have I?'

She laughed. 'You haven't lost a lot of time,' she said. 'We've only known each other for a few months really well.'

'It's not too soon for you?'

'No. I can't believe it, though.'

'Nor me.'

He stood up and pulled her to her feet helping her to straighten her clothes. 'We haven't spoilt this lovely

126

outfit have we?' he asked.

Lee couldn't have cared less if they had but she smoothed her skirts and studied it. It seemed okay.

Then laughing he began to run to the car holding on to her hand. She was laughing and panting and was completely out of breath when they got there and then for good measure he lifted her in his arms and swung her round. 'Oh, Lee, I'm so happy,' he cried.

'Me too,' she said, laughing in delight.

He kissed her again and she told herself that nothing could spoil this happiness, surely. It would be awful if anything happened to spoil it for them. Particularly for Brett who'd already had one disastrous marriage.

They arrived home, eyes sparkling, and full of their good news. Lee's Mum and Dad were delighted to know that she was going to marry Brett. They knew of his first marriage but had got to know him so well they could overlook that and had no fears in accepting him as their future son-in-law. They were sure he would make Lee a good husband and were delighted to see the joy in their daughter's face when they announced their news.

'We must drink to that,' cried Mr. Foster, going to the drinks cabinet. 'If we'd known we would have had champagne in stock.'

'Are your people as delighted as we are?' asked Lee's mother.

'We haven't told them yet,' said Brett, 'but I'm sure they won't be surprised. They know I've been happy since I've met Lee.'

They had been so excited, Lee's Mum and Dad, that they quite forgot to ask how the wedding had gone off and while Brett was telling them all about it Lee went off to find the letter she had so recently received from Des.

And then when the opportunity arose she handed it to him and he read it out loud to them.

'He's got a confounded cheek expecting our Lee to wait for him after what he's done,' said her father.

'That's what I say,' said Brett, 'and because of this I suggested to Lee that we get married right away. Then she can write and tell him and give him plenty of time to get used to the idea while he's inside.'

'Lee hasn't given him any encouragement to go on writing to her or to think that she still cares for him,' said Mr. Foster. 'I told her to ignore his letters and she has done.'

'Well, don't ignore this one, Lee,' said Brett. 'Write and tell him that you are getting married before the end of the month. You can tell him you're sorry and all that but make it quite clear that he means nothing to you any more.'

'I will,' she said, and was glad that Brett knew about the letter which she had been keeping back.

'If he writes again after you've told him you're getting married you can give me the letters to deal with,' he said.

Lee gave a little shudder of fear. Brett seemed so confident that he could deal with Des, but he didn't know the sort of man Des really was.

It seemed that Brett didn't want to leave her that night. Her Mum and Dad had gone to bed ages before he could bring himself to go and she wouldn't have minded if they'd stopped talking until morning. And of course it wasn't all talking, there were kisses and loving and then more talking about their marriage and where they would live until they had a house.

'I haven't wasted the money I received when the house was sold to give Fiona half the value of it,' he said. 'I still have it and the interest has increased it. I'll be able to buy you a nice home.'

'I've got some savings too,' she said. 'I haven't been spending much lately; it will all help.'

He hugged her. 'You're so different from Fiona. I don't think she ever saved a penny in her life.'

At last he managed to tear himself away from her and laughingly told her it was a good thing he'd be getting that special licence immediately. 'I don't think I can hold out much longer now I know that you're going to belong to me.'

And although it was almost time to get up when Lee went to bed she was too excited to sleep. She kept going over and over in her mind all the wonderful things he had said to her this evening. It was unbelievable that she would be married so soon and she wondered where they would live until they had a house ready for them. But it wasn't important where they lived so long as they were together.

She began to make up in her mind a letter to send to Des and because it was impossible to get off to sleep she decided to get up and write it so that it would be off her mind.

She wasn't unkind, she could afford to be nice to him now that things were turning out so well for herself. She told him she thought about him a lot, but she hadn't changed her mind about wanting to marry him and hoped he would be happy for her because she had met someone whom she loved very much. 'I can't live without him,' she wrote, 'and it would be nice if you could give us your blessing.'

She read the letter over anxiously not believing for one moment that he would dream of giving them his blessing, but she was just hoping that by writing to him in that fashion he might accept her rejection of him sensibly and not try to get his own back when he could.

She got back into bed feeling much better after writing the letter and finally she was able to sleep.

6

In the days that followed Lee was so happy she could hardly contain herself. Brett made quite sure that she'd sent her letter off to Des and then he told her to put Des completely from her mind and think only of her future wedding.

And that was quite easy to do. She had very little time in which to get a wedding dress, choose her bridesmaids and get them fixed up and buy all the clothes for her trousseau. She asked her friend Jean, of course, to be a bridesmaid and a cousin of the same height, and young Katie, Mel's daughter, was thrilled to be asked to be bridesmaid again, and then there was a little niece of the same age to match her.

Mel and Sandra were absolutely delighted to know that Brett and Lee were to be married and congratulated themselves on bringing them together in the first place. 'Well, we certainly are grateful to you,' said Brett, 'and always will be.'

And Lee's mother was so happy about it all she was doing all she could to make the wedding a nice one. She bought Lee's wedding dress and the bridesmaids dresses and arranged for a lovely reception to be as nice as Angela's had been and all her family were looking forward to the wedding.

There are always snags and Lee was most disappointed when their vicar wouldn't marry them in the church she had always attended because Brett had been divorced, but he suggested they married at a registry office and then went to church to have the wedding blessed, and that's what they arranged. It upset Brett too, that he couldn't be married to her in church, but she assured him it would make no difference. 'We won't let that spoil anything for us,' she told him.

Angela was delighted to learn, when she returned from her honeymoon, that there was to be another wedding in the family. She, like the rest of Brett's family, was glad to know that he was going to find happiness at last.

It was arranged that they should stay with Lee's Mum and Dad until they had a home of their own. They knew it wouldn't be for long for there were plenty of beautiful houses available. Due to the recession many people who had been in very good positions had been forced out of business or made redundant and their lovely homes were up for sale.

'I suppose this is the best time to be buying property,' said Brett. 'There are some good bargains to be had.'

'Do you regret having to sell your first house?'

'I had no choice,' he said. 'I suppose I could have increased the mortgage in order to give her what she claimed but I didn't really want to do that.'

Lee put her arms around him. 'Poor

Brett. It's a wonder you want to take the plunge again.'

'With you I'd do anything,' he grinned. 'Anyway, it was best to sell everything up and forget that part of my life ever happened.'

Although they were in a hurry to get a home of their own Brett wouldn't make up his mind without careful thought. 'We want to make quite sure we're buying something we really want,' he said, and so they looked round dozens of homes before deciding on one of their choice. Then there was the delay for the solicitors to get the contract through so Brett and Lee were married several weeks before they were able to start getting their home ready for occupation.

But they were happy weeks for both of them. They spent a honeymoon in Minorca, ideal for a honeymoon couple, and they explored the old and new quarters.

Brett hired a car and they were able to see every bit of the island during the two weeks they stayed there. Lots of things would always stand out in their memory. There was the visit to the sanctuary and convent on the summit of the modest mountain, El Toro, and here they were amused to find in the sanctuary, a young man painting the woodwork with a transistor radio at the side of him belting out modern pop tunes. And no one seemed to mind or think it unusual to hear that type of music in such a holy place.

El Toro has been the holy mountain of the island since prehistoric times. From there they viewed the surrounding scenery from a telescope in the sanctuary grounds and got a good view of almost all the island.

They left the sanctuary and the mountain to drive into gorgeous countryside and had a picnic lunch sitting on the huge white rocks so common everywhere in Minorca. The staff at the hotel provided them with some lovely prepacked lunches, more than they could possibly eat, and they sampled the Spanish wines. The sun was gloriously hot and they were content to laze on the slopes and sun bathe.

One evening they visited the Cova D'En Xoroi at Cala En Porter, a cave right on the edge of the cliff where they could drink wine and where there was disco dancing. On the cliff edge was a thick glass window set in the rock through which they could look out across the sea.

Lee felt she was living in a magical world. She would just let her gaze rest on Brett and thought he was the most wonderful person in the world. And she often found him looking at her as if he thought she was the most wonderful girl in the world.

'Happy?' he would ask her, but there was really no need to ask for the happiness shone in her eyes.

They laughed a lot, finding amusement in the most simple things. Lee would go off into peals of laughter when she watched Brett's face when he took a sniff at the goat's milk which was served with their coffee. He was not so adventurous with food as she was. 'I want to sample their cooking,' said Lee, but Brett played safe and ordered English food whenever it was available.

Brett loved mooching round the port of Mahon and the city situated on the cliffs above the port. Here they bought lots of souvenirs to take home with them and presents for various people.

'Are you well off, Brett?' asked Lee one day, for he was extremely generous and didn't seem to have to count the pennies.

He grinned at her. 'That's a question you should have asked before you married me,' he said. 'It's too late to back out if you find I'm not wealthy enough for you.'

'I never thought to ask,' she smiled, and if she had she wouldn't have done because she was happy enough to have Brett with or without riches.

'That's what I like about you,' he said, pulling her close to him. 'I don't think you've asked me to buy you anything while we've been on this holiday. I've never known a girl to be so contented with so little.'

'With so little! I reckon I've got a lot,' she beamed. 'I couldn't be any happier, Brett. You are all I want.'

'Fiona was never satisfied unless I was buying her something all the time. She was like a spoilt baby.'

But because Lee didn't ask for or even hint about any of the beautiful things they saw in the shops it didn't mean that she went without. Brett would have given her anything and he had only to suspect that she liked something and it was here. They had been sure they were right for each other before they were married, but now they were more than sure. They had a perfect relationship.

Brett very rarely mentioned his first wife, it was as if he'd never been married before, and Lee forgot Des Palmer. She and Brett seemed to be isolated on this sunny isle and the rest of the world was very vaguely in the background.

But all good things come to an end and soon it was time to return and start making plans for their future home.

They went to see their solicitor who had prepared the necessary documents for their signatures. The house was in their joint names for Brett said that was the best way to do things. 'Then if I die the house will automatically become yours and vice versa with no further turnover fees to pay.'

'Oh, don't talk about dying, Brett. I've only just got you and I couldn't bear it if we had to part now.'

'Neither could I,' he said, hugging her tight, 'You're a part of me. You're my life.'

'It's true that marriage binds you together. We should be incomplete on our own now,' murmured Lee.

Lee decided to keep her job until she started a family. 'I'd be terribly bored at home all day,' she told Brett, and he quite understood that. She remembered when she had been talking to Des about working after marriage that he had accused her of wanting to go on working because she would miss all the men she worked for if she didn't. There was no nonsense like that with Brett.

She and Brett had been quite happy living with her parents. There had been no snags at all, but the thrill of moving into their own house at last was marvellous. They had as many helpers as Angela and Roger had had for it's fun helping someone to get settled into their new home.

'It's grand to see our Brett happy again,' said Angela. 'I don't know why he was so upset over the breaking up of his marriage to Fiona because she was a little cat. She gave him a hell of a life.'

'He seldom mentions her to me,' said Lee.

'I should think not, and I wouldn't mention it except that I'm so sure that he's completely over her. Mum and Dad are happy too.'

The first day in the house was great.

Lee was in her glory in the kitchen cooking her first Sunday dinner for Brett. Occasionally he came in to see how she was getting on, dipping his finger into this and that to see what it tasted like.

'Go away,' she told him. 'Get on with the gardening. I shall only make a mess of everything if you watch me.'

But then she went out to him to ask him if you had to put an egg with the flour and milk to make a Yorkshire pudding. 'Blessed if I know,' he smirked. 'I should try one and see.'

And her first meal of roast beef with Yorkshire pudding, followed by apple tart and custard pleased him absolutely. He said he'd always liked good English cooking. She had set the table as if setting it for a king and had then sat anxiously opposite him waiting for his verdict and he wouldn't have told her it was terrible if it had been, but he enjoyed it and there were no left-overs.

'That was absolutely delicious,' he said. 'And now I'm too full to do any more gardening.'

'Brett, you know you said you had to entertain people, invite them to dinner?'

'Yes.'

'Well, I don't think I'll be good enough to prepare dinners like that.'

'We'll get someone in to help anyway while you're working,' he said, 'and you'll learn as time goes on. If you served them a meal as good as the one we've just eaten they'd have nothing to grumble about.'

She went and sat on his lap, and put her arms around him. 'You're easy to please,' she said.

'Anyone would be pleased with you, my love,' he smiled. 'And stop stroking my hair like that. You know what it does to me.'

She laughed and he said, 'I don't feel like going out to do any more gardening after that gorgeous meal. Let's go to bed instead.'

'And leave all the washing up?'

'It'll keep,' he said, rising and

drawing her towards the stairs. Well, she was married to him, there was nothing wrong in going to bed with him even if it was the middle of the day. And time flew in his arms. They were expecting visitors to tea and Lee suddenly remembered that the dinner things were waiting to be washed up and put away.

He pulled her down for just one more kiss before letting her go, and shortly afterwards he came down and helped her to clear up and get everything spick and span for their guests to arrive. It was a lovely life having Brett for a husband.

Lee loved her home. It was very similar to Angela's, an executive type house, for Brett, like Roger, wanted a home to be proud of when he invited business people home.

'How have you been managing to entertain these business people since your marriage ended?' asked Lee.

'I used to book a table in a smart restaurant or hotel, even when I was married. It was jolly expensive I can tell you, but I preferred to do that than bring them home, for Fiona was hopeless as a hostess.'

'I hope I don't let you down,' said Lee, anxiously.

'You won't,' he said. 'I have every confidence in you. I know you'd do your best to make visitors welcome and that's the sort of thing that counts.'

After the washing up was done she went quickly round the house to see that everywhere was neat and tidy. Everything was new and she took a terrific pride in it, hating to see a speck of dust anywhere.

The carpets and furniture which they had chosen were of excellent quality and Lee felt she wanted all her friends and the family to come and see what a beautiful home Brett had bought. She vowed she would never let him down. He would always be just as proud as she was to bring friends home and she would learn to be an expert cook. Brett would be glad he'd chosen her for his wife.

As time went on she bought a variety of cookery books and tried out all sorts of exotic meals on Brett who took it all in good part. He liked good plain English cooking but allowed her to experiment on him with her Cordon Bleu cookery and Lee loved experimenting. Brett bought her a deep freezer so that she always had plenty of food in stock in order to try out her culinary skills.

When they gave their first dinner party she was like a cat on hot bricks. Brett, keeping his promise had secured someone to help with the catering, and Lee watched all that she did in order that she could learn to cope on her own. Mrs. Smart, the helper, was delighted to show Lee how to prepare dishes for special occasions such as Avocado stuffed with Crab, Lobster thermidor, Poached Salmon with mayonnaise, and numerous dishes which were carefully entered into Lee's note book for future reference.

Brett often found himself with a most unusual dish put before him for she tried everything out on him before trying it out on the guests and he would sigh in resignation, although he was becoming quite proud of his wife's progress for she was often congratulated on the excellent meals she provided for his special visitors.

Lee was so happy and so busy in her new life she quite forgot to count the weeks to Des Palmer's release from prison and she realised one day that he must have been free for a few weeks and they hadn't heard a thing. He hadn't approached Mel for his job back again or Mel would have told her. She knew Mel worried about what to do if he did ask to return to the firm. For Lee's sake he preferred him to seek employment elsewhere, yet he didn't wish to be unfair to someone who had served his sentence and wanted to make a fresh start.

'Brett,' she said, 'I've only just realised that Des must be out of prison by now. I expected him to get in touch with me as soon as he was out, but I haven't heard a thing.'

'There you are. You worried yourself over nothing.'

'Just fancy. I've had him on my mind for years, dreading the time when he would be able to contact me again, and yet I completely forgot that his time was up when it actually came.'

'Good for you,' he smiled. 'Shows how contented you are.'

'I wonder what he'll do. I shouldn't think he'd have the nerve to come and work with his old work-mates again, should you?'

'Well, I don't know him do I? But I know I wouldn't. I can't imagine how I'd feel in his place. Must be awful.'

'I think I'd kill myself,' said Lee. 'I wouldn't want to go on living.'

'He might find it takes more pluck to kill himself than someone else.'

Lee looked at Brett taking in his handsome profile, his strong masculine body, and he was so dear to her. She had feared that Des would harm whoever she turned to in the future for her happiness and suddenly a cold shiver ran through her at the thought that Des would want to hurt her again through the person she loved. It was a frightening thought which filled her with terror.

She didn't want to worry Brett by asking him to keep a watch out for Des. He had never met Des, of course, but she had shown him pictures of him and she felt like pleading with Brett now to keep a watch out in case he should come anywhere near him. Brett hadn't worried over Des as she'd done because he hadn't experienced the horror that she had.

She tried not to worry and as the days went by she began to feel that perhaps she had no need to for he obviously wasn't seeking her out. But then one day she saw him and nearly jumped out of her skin in fright. She was waiting outside the offices for Brett to pick her up. He was a bit late tonight and there were very few people about. Glancing across the road she found her heart lurch at the familiarity of the man standing watching her. It seemed that time stood still as they looked at each other across the street, and then he began to come towards her and she wondered whether to run for it, but his hands were not in his pockets and he had nothing in them. She was being stupid, and tried to give him a friendly smile as he got nearer.

'Hello, Des,' she said. 'How are you?'

She saw that he was just as handsome as ever, though thinner, and his deep smouldering eyes seemed to have sunk a little into his head, but he was still a very striking man for all that and she realised why she had fallen for him in the beginning.

'Do you care how I am?'

'I've thought about you a lot,' she said, trying to be kind to him.

'You were all I had to think about in there,' he said. 'I proved to you how much I loved you, didn't I?'

151

'Please, Des,' she implored. 'I don't want to talk about that. It made me very ill.'

'And look what it did for me. My whole life ruined. I still love you, Lee.'

'No, Des. You mustn't tell me that. I'm married. I'm happily married. You must accept that. I told you I didn't want our affair to go on. If you could have only accepted that then. And you have to accept it now.'

'I can't accept it. I've always felt that you belonged to me. Why did you marry someone else? I thought you were waiting for me. Why, oh why, Lee, did you have to go and marry someone else?'

'You should have known when I didn't answer your letters that I shouldn't be waiting for you, Des.'

'But you read them, didn't you? I told you so many times how different I would be. You must have known how wretched I was feeling when I couldn't see you for all that time. I prayed that you would come and see me sometime, but you never came. You were very heartless, Lee.'

Lee saw Brett's car turn the corner and said, hastily, 'Here's my husband. Des, I must go.'

'I know. I recognise his car. I've seen him come for you several times.'

'You mean you've been keeping a watch on me?'

'Yes. I wanted to see you. Can't you understand that?'

'But there's no point, Des. I'm married. I can't belong to you and you have to face the fact that I can't.'

As the car got nearer Des turned to go. 'You're hard, Lee,' he said. 'I find it difficult to believe that you could turn against me so much when once you told me how much you loved me.'

He didn't give her an opportunity to say anything else, for Brett had got out of his car and was coming towards her and when she turned to point out Des to him she saw that Des had gone.

'I gather that was Des I saw talking to you,' said Brett, grimly, looking at her face, and seeing fear in her eyes.

'Yes, it was. He said he's seen you coming to pick me up several times. It's uncanny to think that he's been watching us and we weren't aware of it.'

Brett frowned. 'I wish he'd stopped to speak to me and I'd have soon told him to leave you alone.'

'I've made it quite clear that I have put him out of my mind and don't want to be reminded of the past.'

'Let's hope it sinks in,' said Brett, talking her arm to the car.

She was very quiet on the way back home. It seemed that seeing Des had cast a cloud over her. Brett looked at her anxiously. 'You're worried over him, aren't you? He's scared you?'

'I don't like to think we've been watched and that Des is being obstinate in not realising that he's wasting his time. He refuses to accept that I don't want him. He won't believe that I stopped loving him ages ago.'

'He soon disappeared when I came on the scene,' said Brett. 'I'll make damned sure I'm not late again in picking you up. I got caught by old Barker just as I was coming out of the works.'

'Perhaps it's as well that I know he's been hanging around,' said Lee. 'I shall be on the alert in future.'

'I'll get Mel to keep an eye on you,' said Brett. 'I wonder if I should inform the police that Des has been annoying you.'

'I don't think you could say he has been annoying me in the sense they might think you mean. He worried me more than annoyed me. Brett, I'm afraid of him. I'm terrified of what he might do.'

When they arrived home and were indoors Brett took her in his arms. 'My, you are upset, darling. You're trembling. I think I'll get on to the police and ask them to keep an eye on him.'

'It might be as well, Brett. Do you feel scared?'

'I don't like to see you worried. You know you have that look on your face you used to have when I first met you. I have to admit that I don't like it. I thought he would have learned his lesson being locked away for years and that he'd have the sense to keep away from you. The man must be unbalanced.'

'It wouldn't hurt to ask the police to keep an eye on him, I suppose. But how could they keep a watch on him all the time?'

'They couldn't, but I'll give them a ring and mention that he stopped to speak to you outside the works today and that you feel a little apprehensive. We'll tell them that he hasn't threatened you, or anything. He didn't did he?'

'No. He told me I was hard and that he didn't know how I could have married someone else knowing how he felt about me. You couldn't say that was threatening me, but it shows that he still regards me as his possession.'

'Perhaps the police will think we're panicking over nothing, but I'll ring them all the same. They've had more dealings with his sort of character than we've had.'

Lee didn't really think there was much point in getting in touch with the police. Des was crafty, and no doubt he would be able to persuade the police that she was making mountains out of mole hills.

She listened to Brett dialling the station and felt herself trembling. She felt that her lovely life with Brett was threatened and she wanted to scream out in protest. There must be something the police could do to give her peace of mind. She didn't want to get Des into any more trouble; she just wanted to make sure that he left her completely alone in future. She didn't even want to see him let alone talk to him.

7

Lee thought the police might be annoyed with them for wasting their time over what might seem to them something very trivial, but instead they were very understanding and a young policeman came along later to have a talk with them.

'You weren't threatened in any way, Mrs. Lawley?' he enquired.

'No,' Brett answered for her, 'but she has been pestered with letters from him while he was in prison. She ignored most of them, but the last one she didn't. She made it quite clear that she had finished with him before he was sent away and that she was getting married. She was naturally alarmed when he stopped her and reproached her for getting married which is understandable considering the way he behaved when he saw her with any

158

other man before.'

The young policeman agreed. 'We have these problems all the time. Sending a man to prison doesn't necessarily mean that's the end of the problem, but we haven't sufficient men to be able to watch every released man in order to prevent him attacking again, though we do our best. You say that Des Palmer stopped your wife outside the place where she works?'

'That's right, I happened to be late picking her up and he told her he had seen me, he recognised my car, and it's worrying to know we're being watched by a man like him.'

'It's quite likely then that he will be there again spotting a chance to talk to you, Mrs. Lawley. We will keep some sort of supervision for a time, at least. It's not right that you should live in terror.'

'I don't want him to start pestering her here, either,' said Brett. 'I shall make quite sure she isn't left on her own.'

'It does seem you will have to be on the alert for a time. See how things go. You don't want me to go and have a word with him?'

'That might antagonise him,' said Lee. 'He hasn't actually done anything wrong, has he? It's just that I didn't like him approaching me and we did feel we should get in touch with the police in case he tries anything again, although we realise that you can't be watching us twenty-four hours of the day.'

'For a time, until we're certain that he isn't going to try any tricks, we'll keep our eyes on him as much as possible,' said the young policeman, and they realised that there was nothing else they could do.

Neither Brett nor Lee felt like much to eat — Brett because he was concerned over Lee who looked very pale and frightened — so after a snack they went round to see Mel and Sandra.

'Your nerves will be shattered again, Lee,' said Sandra, 'imagining that that dreadful man might pounce again.'

'I'm only just beginning to realise myself what a cloud of fear Lee has been living under all the time I've known her. I can't say that I like the thought of being watched by a murderer,' said Brett, 'and I shall have no peace whenever I am not with Lee.'

'I'll see that she never leaves the works again on her own,' said Mel. 'I'll keep you under my nose as much as possible,' he smiled at her. 'I wonder what he's doing for a living. He hasn't applied for his job back again.'

'Perhaps he's not doing anything yet,' said Lee. 'He won't be short of money for a bit because he had saved a lot towards the marriage which didn't come off. He can't have a regular job because he recognised Brett's car and told me he had seen him calling for me. He's had his eyes on us for some time.' She shuddered at the thought.

'It's dreadful that someone can make your life hell,' said Sandra. 'Do make sure that there's always someone with you.'

Brett was scared for Lee's safety and she was just as scared for his. She felt that Des was more likely to attack the man she loved rather than herself, for he had attacked Roy, not her.

Mel and Sandra played some tapes and did their best to take their minds off the matter for a time and before long Lee had almost persuaded herself that they were being too dramatic. Everything would be all right. If Des had wanted to harm them he could have done it before now because hadn't he admitted that he'd been watching her and Brett.

Sitting nice and cosy in their friends' lounge exchanging news, discussing the case of that little boy who'd gone to America, and all sorts of things, it was difficult to imagine that there is so much wickedness in the world. But for all Mel and Sandra had tried to take their minds off Des all the evening they were concerned for them, for Mel told

Brett to make quite sure that Des wasn't lurking in the grounds of their home when they got back. 'I don't want to add to your fears, but it is best to be on your guard. He can be dangerous and at least you won't be taken unawares as Roy was. I believe Roy was a judo expert but Des got him because the attack was so absolutely unexpected.'

When they arrived home Lee didn't move from Brett's side while he locked the car and they walked from the garage into their house. And then when they were safely inside Brett suddenly took her in his arms and held her tight. 'I could kill him,' he said, fiercely. 'If he harms you I will kill him, I swear.'

'We were so happy,' she said. 'Why can't he leave us alone?'

'Nothing's going to spoil it for us,' he said. 'He won't get a chance to get either of us.'

Lee was glad to be at work with plenty of people the next day. If she'd been left at home on her own she would have been frightening herself to death imagining that Des would come and get her there.

It was reassuring when she left the office with Mel, who waited outside with her until Brett arrived, to see a police constable walking slowly up and down across the way from the offices. He didn't approach her, making it obvious that he was keeping a watch on her, but it was very comforting to know that the police were at hand to protect the public wherever possible.

There was no sign of Des and she turned to Mel with an apologetic smile. 'All this fuss for nothing,' she said. 'No sign of him.'

'Best to be on the safe side. Take no chances. Maybe he's seen the copper over the way.'

After a few days like that Lee began to feel calmer. She had seen no sign of Des, perhaps he had seen the police-man and had been scared away, or had realised that she could not belong to him now because she was married to

Brett and had decided to give up as a bad job.

After a week or so she noticed that the policeman was not outside the works any more so they must have considered at the station that vigilance was no longer necessary and Lee began to breathe a little more freely.

It made a great difference not having to sleep on her own each night worrying as she had done before her marriage to Brett. She had her husband to love her to sleep so she didn't spend sleepless nights worrying.

There were times when she was out that she would have a queer feeling that she was being watched and would look all around apprehensively, but never saw a sign of Des and put it all down to her imagination. She supposed it would be years before she could outgrow her fear of him.

And then sometimes when she shut her eyes at night she could quite clearly see those deep-set eyes, brooding and smouldering, and would feel his presence very close. It was uncanny and she wondered if he was awake thinking of her and that she was picking up his thoughts.

Brett seemed to have been able to dismiss Des from his thoughts for he never mentioned him, though he never went out at night and left her on her own even for a short time. Inevitably there were times when he had to go out and see people on business and on these occasions he would either arrange for her to have visitors to keep her company, or would drop her off perhaps for an hour with Mel and Sandra, Angela and Roger, or her parents where he knew she'd be safe, and he'd pick her up later.

For one night a week Lee had arranged to go with Jean to a cookery class. Jean was getting married soon to Dave who had been with them on that awful Sunday, and when she admitted to Lee that she could do with some tuition as she could do little more than boil an egg, Lee offered to take some lessons with her and they were finding them very interesting.

Brett always took them to the evening institute and collected them later, making quite sure he was on time and waiting for them inside the building. He pulled their legs about their cooking, telling Jean that he had never suffered so much from indigestion in his life, but he was always ready to sample the dishes they had cooked during the evening and admitted seriously that Lee was becoming a superb cook and that he was very proud to invite anyone home these days.

When Lee knew that Jean was going to marry Dave she couldn't help wondering whether she would have become serious with Roy after that outing if Des hadn't come and taken his life. She would no doubt have gone on making up a foursome with Dave and Jean if Roy had wanted that, and they had got on very well for the short time they'd been together, though there hadn't been enough time to find out very much about him.

But then she would look at Brett and felt that she wouldn't have fallen in love with Roy. She and Brett just belonged together and fate had intended them to meet, but had gone a very peculiar way of getting them together for if there had been no tragedy Mel would not have felt protective towards her or felt anxiety to get her back to work again, and without Mel she would never have met his cousin Brett for it was he who had planned to get them together knowing how they would suit each other. It was said that out of evil cometh good and meeting Brett had been the best thing that had ever happened to her.

They had many friends now. Never a week went by without their being invited to some party, or Lee giving a dinner party at their home. On some evenings Brett would bring a pile of work home with him which he had been too busy to cope with during the day and she would give him a hand with it. Often she spent an hour or two typing letters and reports for him.

And then of course the families on both sides took up a lot of their time. They went visiting his parents, her parents, seeing her brothers and their families, and keeping in touch with Angela and Roger. They were a very busy couple with no time to become bored and their friends were numerous. Brett had no cause to complain that he was ashamed to bring his friends home now as he'd been when he was married to Fiona, for Lee took a lot of pride in their home.

Brett gave her plenty of money to run the home; she never had to ask him for any, and he insisted that the money she earned herself was her own to spend as she liked and so she had the pleasure of buying herself lovely clothes. She had never had so much money to spend on herself before, and had never possessed such a large variety of clothes all of good quality so that she could dress for all occasions, but at week-ends she was generally to be seen in her old jeans and a jumper or shirt helping Brett in the garden and looking a completely different person from the one who went out well dressed to meet friends, or stayed at home to welcome visitors. And she loved to see Brett pottering around doing odd jobs here and there in his old slippers and wearing jeans like herself.

Although they had considered the house perfect when they bought it Brett was always finding ways of improving it; fixing cupboards here, changing the décor in this room or that. The gardens were a picture. They would often take a run out in the car to some nurseries and pick up delightful plants or trees to add to the beauty of the gardens back and front.

They both enjoyed gardening when the weather was fit to work outside. Close to the house were lovely flower beds, and they were planning to have fruit trees in one section, a kitchen garden in another, for Lee was anxious to try growing herbs.

They had decided to wait at least a year before starting a family. 'We'll have a year all for ourselves,' said Brett, 'and then we'll see what happens.'

The year was almost up and Lee felt it time to think about children now for Brett was older than herself and she knew he had longed for children when he had married before but Fiona hadn't wanted any.

They had not seen nor heard anything from Des since that time he had spoken to her outside the offices and they felt safe enough now to make plans for a family. Lee didn't think she'd any longer be afraid to stay at home while Brett was at work. Perhaps Des had seen that policeman on patrol after their meeting and had realised he was being watched and wouldn't contact her again.

Once Lee had made up her mind she wanted to start a family she found herself looking at little children every-where and trying to imagine what her own children would be like. They had furnished two of their bedrooms only, the other two remained carpetless and without furniture. Lee had been tidying the bedrooms when Brett came and stood in the second-best bedroom looking round, and Lee said, 'Do you feel as I do, that these rooms are waiting to be occupied?'

He smiled at her. 'Is that how you feel?'

'Yes. Do you?'

'I suppose I do. We are very happy but I do have that feeling that we have children waiting to join us.'

'That's exactly how I feel,' she said, dreamily, and he caught her in his arms. 'You want to start a family?'

'H'm, h'm. I do.'

'It's okay by me,' he said, still holding her close. 'Let's try our luck.'

'Not right this minute,' she laughed, pushing him away. 'I'm busy.'

'There's no time like the present,' he declared, with a cheeky grin.

She was glad he wanted to start a

family as much as she did for there were girls who worked with her whose husbands weren't keen to have children for they were enjoying life while their wives were working and there were no children to prevent their going out for a good time in the evening.

Lee wasn't the type who wanted to go out every evening. She enjoyed company but also being at home just with Brett and he seemed contented to spend evenings at home with her when they were not entertaining or being entertained. She was sure neither of them would mind having to give up lots of other pleasures in order to have the pleasure of children. And she was fortunate that Brett never wanted to leave her in the evenings to go out drinking with the boys. If he went out he took her with him.

Now that they had made up their minds not to delay, Lee became most anxious in case they shouldn't be successful. She was so eager to please Brett in every way it would be terrible if she wasn't able to give him children.

But quite soon after their decision was made Lee thought she might have conceived. She was afraid to say anything for the time being but it was a secret she was having great difficulty in keeping, for she felt it would have been a shame to boost Brett's belief that she was going to have a baby if it was just a false alarm.

It was Sandra who first noticed the difference in her. 'Are you all right, Lee?' she asked, one night after she and Mel had spent an evening with Lee and Brett.

'Yes,' said Lee. 'I feel rather sleepy these days, I must admit, but I'm okay, really.'

'You're not having a baby, are you?'

Brett looked at her swiftly and Lee found the colour rushing to her face. 'I might be,' she admitted.

'I'll bet you are,' said Sandra. 'I recognise the look. Have you started having morning sickness?'

'No,' said Lee. 'But I don't feel so

good when I get up these mornings.'

'Oh, you'll be starting morning sickness,' exclaimed Sandra, delightedly, 'and then you'll know for sure.'

When she saw the way Brett was looking at Lee, Sandra put her hand to her mouth. 'Oh, gosh, Lee. I've opened my big mouth too soon, haven't I? You haven't told Brett, yet?'

'I wanted to be sure.'

'Sandra!' cried Mel. 'That's something Lee would have wanted to tell Brett when they were alone. It's their secret.'

'Sorry, Brett,' said Sandra. 'I'm afraid having had three children I'd forgotten how exciting it is when you know for the first time that you are going to have a baby. Sorry.'

'You haven't spoilt the excitement at all, Sandra,' cried Brett. 'If it's true Lee, I'm over the moon.'

He went to her and hugged her close. 'Is it?'

'I'm not really sure yet,' she said, her eyes alight. 'But it could be.'

He turned to the others, proudly. 'We planned for it, you know.'

Mel laughed, congratulating Brett because he was to become a father. 'We planned for our first, but not the other two.'

'Oh. Mel,' cried Sandra, 'we wouldn't do without them.'

'Not now we have them,' he agreed.

'But you would have done before? Oh, Mel, I thought you were delighted about having the other two.'

'Stop looking alarmed, darling. I'm just as thrilled with our little dears as you are.'

He called them the little dears as if they were anything but and seeing Sandra's expression he laughed, and planted a kiss on her face.

Brett was holding on to Lee so tight and giving her such loving looks she did wish they'd been alone when he had learned the news.

'Oh, I'm so thrilled for you, Lee,' said Sandra.

'I'm not sure,' said Lee, once again.

'I know you're pregnant,' said Sandra. 'I can tell the look.'

'I wonder how she could tell,' Lee asked Brett on the way home.

'It must be the joy you are radiating,' he said. 'I shall be radiating it myself now that I know, and the people at work will be asking me if I'm going to have a baby.'

'Idiot,' she laughed.

When they arrived home he kept looking at her with a smile, quite bemused. 'I can't believe it,' he said. 'You'll take care, won't you? You won't be going to work any more, will you?'

'Oh, I will, Brett. I shall be able to work for quite a while. It will make the time pass more quickly for me. I'm really impatient.'

In bed he held her tight. 'Wonder what it will be, a boy or a girl,' he said.

'It's bound to be one or the other,' she laughed, mischievously.

'One of each, perhaps.'

'Oh, you. I don't know how I'll get on having one, let alone two. Besides, we can't be too sure.'

'We can. You said you could be and Sandra recognises the symptoms, whatever they are.'

He began to kiss her and said, 'It's good for a pregnant woman to have as much love as possible.'

'You've just made that up,' she giggled.

'It's bound to be true, though,' he laughed, and because they both believed it they decided to end the evening with a nice loving session.

Lee hugged her secret at work. She didn't want to tell anyone her good news until she was absolutely certain but she didn't feel her normal self. Great waves of tiredness engulfed her at times, and then came the first morning that she was sick. It was a horrible feeling, but as soon as it was over she rushed downstairs to tell Brett.

'Brett! Brett! It must be right. I've just been horribly sick.'

'Oh, you poor thing,' he said, sympathetically.

'I've been waiting for morning sickness to start,' she said, brushing aside his sympathy. 'Now there's no doubt about it. We're going to have a baby. Oh, Brett, I'm so thrilled.'

'So am I, darling. I wish I could be with you all the time now to see that you take care. I shall hate to have to leave you all day.'

'Other men have to leave their wives,' she said. 'You won't have time to get tired of me, not seeing me all day long.'

'I'll never be tired of you, sweetheart,' he promised.

He dropped her off at work and she could see he didn't want to leave her. 'I'll be earlier today, Lee. We have to go to the Foresters, remember?'

'Of course.'

But she felt so tired during the day she wondered if she would have the energy to go out in the evening. Mel laughed when he saw her after lunch. 'I think you'd better go and have a lie down in the rest room,' he said, 'or you'll be falling asleep at your desk.'

'Oh, dear, I'm sorry, Mel,' she said. 'I've never felt like this before.'

He laughed. 'You've never been pregnant before.'

'Did Sandra feel tired when she was expecting?'

'Yes. I believe it affects a lot of women like that. At least Sandra tells me it does.'

The tiredness wore off and when Brett called for her Lee was feeling quite lively and able to go out and meet the Foresters.

'We shan't need a great deal to eat,' said Brett. 'Myra always puts on a good spread and it's a shame not to have an appetite when she's gone to all that trouble.'

Lee laughed. 'You needn't worry about my appetite,' she said. 'I can't stop eating.'

'Because you have to feed the baby too, or is it because you are sick and need to fill up again?'

'Oh, Brett,' she said, 'you make me feel horrible.'

But they were both laughing and he said she'd been on his mind all day. 'I felt like telling everyone at work that I'm going to become a father soon,' he told her.

'What shall I do?' she asked, when they arrived home. 'I have some ham and I'll make a salad. That won't be too filling will it?'

'That will suit me fine,' he said.

He always helped her prepare the meal when they got back from work. She put the kettle on while he set the table, and she was wondering what to wear for the evening. She had plenty of clothes to choose from and she was trying to remember what outfit she wore the last time she saw the Foresters, she didn't want to wear the same again.

'Oh, damn!' said Brett.

'What's the matter?' she asked.

'I intended to get some petrol for the car. I'll just nip off and get some while you finish the salad just in case the garage closes early. It

181

won't take me long.'

He went off to fetch the car keys and soon she heard him driving away, and carried on with her preparations for the meal.

She switched on the television and was busy watching the news when she thought she heard the kitchen door open, but she hadn't heard Brett's car return and in any case, he hadn't had time to get to the garage and back yet.

Perhaps he had forgotten his wallet and she called, 'That you, Brett?'

But there was no answer and she thought it must have been just her imagination that she'd heard someone come in. She watched something of interest on the television and then went off into the kitchen for some cutlery.

It hadn't been her imagination that someone had come into the kitchen and her heart stood still, for it wasn't Brett standing there it was Des Palmer.

8

'What are you doing here?' Lee cried, in alarm.

'I've come to talk to you.'

'You'd better go quickly. Brett's only slipped out for some petrol.'

'He never leaves you on your own, does he?'

'So you've been keeping an eye on us?'

'Yes. I've watched the house night after night, but he's always here with you, or you go out together. But he's slipped up tonight.'

'How did you know we lived here?'

'I've followed you from work, many times, and I've hung around waiting for him to go out and leave you alone.'

'He'll be back any minute. What do you want?'

'You. I want you to come with me. Now, before he gets back. If you don't

I'll kill him. I have a gun, see.' He produced one and pointed it at her.

Lee felt her inside trembling. Her greatest fear was for Brett. Supposing he came back and was taken unawares as Roy was. 'All right, I'll come with you. But you promise you only want to talk to me?'

'Yes. My car is just round the bend. We can go to it and talk there undisturbed.'

She didn't like the look in his eyes, but she was so terribly afraid for Brett and also for herself as she allowed him to take her to his car. She wished Brett would return while they were walking down the drive. He'd have a chance to see them together and know there was something wrong and perhaps he could outwit Des, yet at the same time she prayed he wouldn't come yet, not while Des had that gun in his hand for Brett would stand no chance against that and she was quite sure Des would use it.

When she reached his car he opened the door for her to get in and she didn't see that she had any option but to obey. He got into the driving seat, leaned over to lock the door on her side and then turned the key in the ignition to start up.

'What are you doing?' she cried, full of fear. 'You said you only wanted to talk to me.'

'I do. And I have a place where we can talk undisturbed. You don't think I'm going to risk being seen with you, do you?'

She clasped her hands in her lap to try and stop herself from trembling. She remembered that she was pregnant and told herself she must keep calm because of the baby. No harm must come to the little one.

'You informed the police that I came to speak to you, didn't you?' he said.

'We wanted to be left alone,' she replied.

'I saw the policeman keeping watch and I've had enough of the police and prison officers. I lay low for a bit until you all thought I'd given up trying to contact you, but I have waited so long to talk to you, Lee. Waited so long for us to be alone again.'

'But there's no point, Des. I'm married. If you thought anything of me at all you'd be glad to know that I'm happy.'

'Thought anything of you? I've been in jail for years because of you! It was because I loved you that I couldn't bear you to be with anyone else.'

'Your love was selfish, Des. You wanted me just for yourself and wouldn't share me with anyone, not even my family.'

She was trying to talk reasonably, not wishing to upset him in any way. He was showing no remorse for what he'd done, in fact he seemed rather proud of it, mentioning it to prove to her that he loved her. What did they call a person who showed no remorse for his crimes? A psychopath?

'I wanted you to belong to me entirely,' he said. 'Can't you understand? You're the only person in the world I want to be with. And all the time I was locked away I looked forward to the time when I could be with you again to tell you what I'd gone through for you. You don't think it was pleasant in there, do you?'

'Of course I don't. I used to think about you a lot. But then I thought about Roy and the way his family were feeling. You broke their hearts, Des.'

'I warned you not to go with anyone else. I told you that if I couldn't have you no one else would and I meant it, and I proved that I meant it.'

She noticed that they were travelling along winding narrow lanes. 'Where are you taking me?' she asked, trying not to sound afraid.

'I'm keeping off the main roads,' he said. 'By now that man of yours will have discovered that you have disappeared and he'll guess that I've picked you up. He will notify the police and they'll be looking for my car so I'm keeping away from all built-up areas. Of course it will take us a lot longer to get there, but that doesn't matter now that you're with me.'

'To get where?' she asked.

He turned to smile at her. 'Full of curiosity, aren't you? I've bought a little cottage in a very remote part of Wales. I like it there because you rarely see any people. I thought you and I could be alone there to talk without disturbances.'

'Des, prove that you love me by taking me back home. Brett will be in a terrible state. This can't do any good, snatching me away from home. Please, Des,' she pleaded.

'I'm not taking you back home. I want you to stay with me.'

'In a remote little spot all on our own?'

'Yes.'

'That's what you always wanted, wasn't it? To get me away where I couldn't talk to anyone but you?'

'That's right. I've got used to my own company and I don't want anyone else's. I never did want anyone else's, not even my mother's and father's company. I like to be on my own, and there was never anyone else I wanted to be with until I met you.'

'Are you hoping to keep me with you indefinitely?'

'I believe that when we have been together again for a little while you'll want to stay with me. You loved me once and I'll make you love me again.'

'And supposing I still want to return to my husband?'

'You won't. Lee, can't you feel that we belong together?'

She didn't answer. She knew that she belonged to Brett and could imagine herself with no one else in the world. It was a tragedy if Des felt that he belonged to her and she to him, and he couldn't be happy with anyone else. She was sorry about it. She couldn't imagine anything worse than to discover that Brett no longer needed her. It gave her sympathy for Des, and for all other people who felt they couldn't do without the one they loved, and wondered what fate was playing at in making one person love another who was not meant for him. She supposed it was all very well to say people should pull themselves together, but it would be like the end of the world to her if anything happened to Brett.

But people had lost their beloveds and pulled through. Des was making no effort. It was not love for her he was feeling, but a determination not to be beaten. 'If I died, Des,' she said, 'You would have to get over it and find someone else to share your life with you.'

'If you had died,' he said. 'I would have died with you.'

She looked at him in disbelief and he smiled. 'People do kill themselves when they lose someone they love as much as themselves.'

They travelled on and on and she knew it would be ages before they came to Wales on these minor roads. She thought of the meal she had been preparing and the Foresters waiting for them to go to them for a meal and the thought of food made her realise how hungry she was.

'Des, can't we stop somewhere for something to eat?'

'I've plenty of food,' he said. 'I think we're far enough away now to stop for a little while.'

As soon as he found a gateway to a farm he pulled in to it, leaving room in case another car should come along the lane and want to pass them.

She knew that while he was looking for the food she could get out of the car and run for her life but how far would she get before he caught her? He'd got a gun and it would be too risky to try and escape in this quiet country lane for there wasn't a soul to come to her rescue.

She supposed the best thing she could do was to be friendly with Des, not oppose him in any way, and eventually she would be rescued. The police would be searching for her when Brett reported that she was missing.

Poor Brett. She could just imagine the state he was in at the moment.

From the boot of his car Des fetched a carton filled with food of all descriptions. 'You see I'm well prepared,' he said. 'I knew that as soon as I got the chance to get you on your own I should persuade you to come to the cottage with me and so I've always carried plenty of food in the car.'

He hadn't persuaded her to come, she thought, he'd forced her. She had had no choice.

'I've been very patient,' he went on. 'I've watched your house so many times in the hope that your husband would leave you alone one night, and I've eaten food in the car while I've been waiting.' He smiled, 'It helped to pass the time away. I knew if I could just get you on your own it would be easy.'

If only they'd known that it was his car parked nearby, thought Lee. This was a new car, she couldn't have known it belonged to him if she'd seen it. No wonder she had felt his presence near to her so many times.

'What are you doing for a living?' she asked, as he passed her a buttered roll with cheese filling.

'While I was in jail I took up writing. I have written quite a lot of short stories for boy's magazines under a pen name. I've written some of those scripts for picture stories, a job I don't particularly like, but the pay is good and it keeps me going. I've been having a go at drawing illustrations for the scripts as well and the publishers seem to be pleased with them. I'll show them to you when we get to the cottage.'

'And you think that's the way you will earn your living in future?'

'Yes. I don't have to see people, there's no one to ask questions, and I have an ambition to write thrillers. The life would suit me fine — living in the cottage and you living with me.'

'How long have you had the cottage?'

From a flask he poured some coffee which Lee accepted thankfully. 'I've had my eye on the cottage for some time. It needed a lot of renovation so I got it dirt cheap and I've had it all put in good condition. I've been working on it myself as well as employing builders. It's only been ready a week or so. Just in time,' he smiled.

'Have your Mum and Dad seen it?'

'No. They know I've bought a cottage but I haven't told them where. I intended to bring you out here as soon as I got the chance and it was better that they didn't know where it was. The police will be asking them questions and they won't be able to answer them.'

He handed Lee another buttered roll with boiled ham this time and he gave her a tomato and some lettuce. She ate the food and enjoyed it, wondering how she could do so when he was supplying it.

She watched Des eating too. He was far more handsome than Brett and yet nothing near so attractive because his dark eyes had a sullen look in them most of the time and he had no humour in him as Brett had. When Brett was teasing her and laughing with her she thought he was the most wonderful looking man in the world.

Des produced some iced buns to round off their meal and when they'd finished he set off again towards the cottage. Lee was very quiet, thinking how strange it was that she was sitting here at his side and making no fuss. But if she had screamed and tried to attract attention there was no knowing what he would have done. She believed he was insane. It was a dreadful thought to know she was with someone out of his mind, but he must be mad to think he could get away with kidnapping her like this. Surely there was no place in England where he could hide her away indefinitely. The only thing she could do was to play along with him until she found an opportunity to get away safely.

They travelled on and on and when it became dark Lee grew tired and allowed herself to drop off to sleep. When she awoke she saw that they were right in the wilds. Houses were scattered here and there but they were very few and far between.

'You've had a nice sleep,' said Des. 'We haven't much further to go. I would have made it much sooner if I could have kept to the main roads, but we shall be there soon now.'

'Do you think I could ring through to Brett and tell him I'm all right to stop his worrying?'

'No, you can't!' Des snapped, angrily. 'They might be able to trace where the call came from, the area, and then they'd know where to start looking for you.'

'Don't you care about causing misery to other people?'

'You can talk! What about the misery you've caused me? There would have been no misery for anyone if you hadn't behaved as you did, declaring that you didn't love me any more after all we'd been to each other. I was going to buy you a lovely home and I'd have been good to you. It was you who spoilt it all. You start thinking of me now, and forget all about Brett.'

It was no use talking to him. He was convinced that she was in the wrong and that he had the right to claim her like this. What was going to come of it all?

Soon they came to what was little more than a cart track. 'Is the cottage along here?' she asked.

'Yes. Quite a long way off the beaten track, isn't it?'

It was and her heart sank. Who would ever find her here?

It was a long track to the cottage and the car rocked crazily on the uneven surface, making them jerk in all directions, and then it opened out on to a yard in front of a solid greystone cottage.

Des went driving on and she saw in the darkness a shed looming towards them. He got out, unlocked the doors and drove the car inside. 'Come along,' he said, 'the car will be out of sight in here in case anyone comes snooping around.'

He handed her the carton of food and other things from the car and told her to go ahead, but he lingered to lock up the doors of the shed. He directed her to the cottage which looked cold and forbidding in the darkness, but she had no doubt it would look entirely different in daylight.

He unlocked the door and gave her a nudge to go inside. They went through a kitchen which, to her surprise, looked fitted out in a modern style considering the age of the cottage, and then they went through into the sitting-room which was also furnished quite pleasantly. Des had good taste if he'd chosen the furniture, which wasn't new but of good quality.

'Put the things down,' he said, for Lee was still clutching them in her arms, and as she did so he switched on the electric fire.

'Electricity in this isolated spot,' she commented.

'Yes. We aren't all that far away from civilization,' he smiled.

'It seems as if we are in the back of beyond.'

'You'll find it very comfortable here. The place grows on you.'

She sincerely hoped the house didn't grow on her, that she wouldn't be here long enough for that, and felt very near to bursting into tears. He looked at her and said, savagely, 'Don't cry.'

He went off into the kitchen and put the kettle on. 'I think a drink, a little snack and bed,' he said. 'We'll talk in the morning.'

She looked at him in alarm. Was he hoping to sleep with her? The tears did fall now. She felt so helpless and afraid and kept thinking about Brett. If only she could have given him a ring to let him know she was okay, and could hear his comforting voice on the phone.

She was glad of the hot coffee and ate another buttered roll with some cheese. He watched her eating with satisfaction. 'You're going to make yourself at home?' he asked.

It was late and she thought it best to humour him, for the moment anyway. 'It is homely here,' she said.

'Isn't it? I've enjoyed getting it all ready for you.'

'You were so sure you would be able to get me to come?'

'I knew I had to wait for my chance but I was quite confident the time would come.'

Lee shuddered at the thought of his watching her and Brett for so long, and she thought of those horrible moments when she had felt herself being watched.

She studied Des sitting there across the table with a complacent look on his face and wondered what he had done with the gun, and when he arose she saw it tucked into the belt of his trousers. He didn't intend to be caught unawares without it. If only she could get possession of it. But what would she do then? Shoot him? What would they do to her if she did?

She felt dreadfully weary after the

long hours of travelling and she saw that Des was looking tired too. That was a good thing. She wanted him to be too weary to try and take advantage of her tonight and prayed that before tomorrow night she would have been found. She was afraid to mention anything about going to bed or where she would sleep and was prepared to sit up all night rather than sleep with him, tired as she was.

He seemed to enjoy sitting there, just watching her. Like a cat with a mouse, she thought, and began to fidget under his scrutiny. He smiled. 'You don't know how I have longed to be able to sit and just look at you and know you are mine,' he said.

Fear ran through her. 'Would it give you pleasure to possess someone who doesn't want to be possessed?' she asked.

He laughed and then said, 'Yes, it would. It would give me a lot of pleasure to possess someone who doesn't want to be possessed. But in the end you will want me as much as I want you.'

She didn't answer and he said, 'Come on, you must be tired. I expect you want to know where you will sleep.'

That didn't sound so bad. He had said where *you* will sleep not where *we* will sleep.

He took her upstairs. She had no night clothes. She had nothing but what she stood up in, for he hadn't given her time even to put on a coat. There were two bedrooms in the cottage and she was glad to see there was a bathroom too. 'The water is hot as I switched the immersion heater on when we came in,' he said. 'We have our own water supply.'

Then he showed her the room where she was to sleep. It was only a small room containing a single bed and bare necessities. That was a relief. He couldn't very well share a single bed with her, a big fellow like him.

She paused outside the bathroom

and said, 'Well, goodnight, Des.'

'Goodnight,' he smiled, and she slipped into the bathroom finding her heart was thumping rapidly. She couldn't believe her luck that she wasn't expected to sleep with him. Now she stood there thinking this was the first time she had been alone since he'd picked her up from the house. It was like a dream.

She looked round the bathroom. No chance of escape from here. It contained only a small window and she doubted whether she could get through it even if she could reach up to it. She was too tired to bother a great deal with her toilet. She washed her teeth and swilled her face quickly and when she left the bathroom she nearly jumped out of her skin. Des was waiting outside.

'I thought you'd gone downstairs,' she said.

'No,' he said. 'I have to keep you in sight, my dear. I'm going to lock your bedroom door.'

'There's no need for that,' she cried. 'Supposing I need to go to the bathroom in the night.'

'You'll have to call,' he said, unperturbed.

'Don't lock me in,' she pleaded. 'I shall have such a dreadful feeling if I know I'm locked in that small room.'

'That's what I thought. You can't imagine what it's like to be locked up until it happens to you. Night after night I was locked in a prison cell and I want you to know what I went through for you.'

She looked at him, horrified. 'You're going to keep me like a prisoner here?'

'Not all the time.'

'Oh, Des, you said you only wanted to talk to me.'

'Yes. I want to tell you what it was like over the years when we were apart, and I want you to experience the awful feeling you get when the key is turned in the lock.'

She didn't move towards the bedroom, but he pushed her forward. 'Go on,' he said.

'Please don't lock me in,' she cried. 'Please, Des.'

'That's how we all felt in prison,' he said. 'But no one cared.'

'You say you love me.'

'I do. And when you know how I suffered perhaps you will be sorry you spoilt everything between us and will be contented to stay with me.'

He gave her a push into the room and she clung to the door, but what hope had she against a man of his strength? She was forced into the room and then the door was shut and she heard the key turn in the lock.

It was more than Lee could stand. She had managed to keep some sort of control over herself until now, but the sound of the key turning in the lock, making her a prisoner, drove her to despair and she sank down behind the door in a storm of weeping.

A knock came on the door and she

listened. 'Tears don't do any good at all,' he said, and she knew he was outside there listening to her. The callous devil.

'Tomorrow night I might let you sleep with me,' he said, and she knew that was not a promise but a threat.

And of course tears didn't do any good so she pulled herself together and began to look around. There was a bedside lamp to light the room and she saw that the window had tiny square panes only one of which opened at the top to let in fresh air so it was no use thinking she could break the glass or open the window and get through there. It really was like being in a prison cell with no possible chance of escape.

She lay on the bed feeling exhausted and too ill to bother to undress even if she had nightclothes with her. She began to feel cold and pulled the bedclothes around her. Surprisingly with the warmth given by the adequate covering she went off to sleep far sooner than she would have expected and awoke next morning feeling sick and needing to go to the bathroom. She couldn't hear a sound and didn't know what time it was. She banged on the door and fortunately Des came without delay and she went rushing off to the bathroom.

She stayed in the bathroom for ages hating to go out and see Des waiting, for she was sure he would be there, but he had gone downstairs and called to her, 'Breakfast is ready.'

'Am I allowed to come downstairs?' she asked.

'Yes, I'm not bringing your breakfast up to you.'

Thankfully she went down and he was busy putting out bacon and an egg for her. 'Have you had yours?' she asked.

'No, it's here,' he said, taking another plate from under the grill and putting it on the table. She saw that it was all prepared very nicely and there was lightly fried bread which she loved.

'Did you sleep well?' he asked.

'Yes, thank you,' she muttered, and was afraid to complain about being locked in in case he should suggest again that she slept with him tonight, that would be the worst of two evils.

When they had finished breakfast she got up to wash the breakfast things and looked from the window to see that the cottage stood in its own grounds which were quite extensive. If she managed to get out of the place there was that long track back to the quiet country lane and he could follow her in the car and bring her back in no time. But she wasn't going to give up hope. There must be some way to escape.

Des was watching her and seemed to read her thoughts. 'I shan't give you a chance to leave me,' he said, 'so it's no use thinking of ways to get away. I'm going into town for some provisions this morning and you will be safely locked in your room.'

She gave him a look of appeal which was entirely wasted and as soon as the washing up was done he ordered her back up the stairs and she had no option but to obey him. He had shown no violence towards her yet but she had no doubt that he would if she tried to oppose him in any way.

'Year in and year our I was locked up,' he said. 'I want you to know what it was like for a little time and then you will sympathise with me. Just think of the years being locked away like an animal. There were times when I wanted you so badly, and other times I hated you, Lee. I longed to punish you for spoiling our lives.'

Back in the bedroom locked in for goodness knows how long Lee sat on the bed in despair. She was being punished for daring to stop loving a man who was a tyrant.

Now she was at his mercy and she was sure he had no compassion in him. Her tears couldn't move him and he didn't care a toss what she went through. In fact he was enjoying tormenting her. He had never loved her. He had wanted to possess her, as some people like to possess animals, and he wanted her to be obedient, do everything he wanted her to.

She sat with her head in her hands and wondered how long it would be before she was discovered here, if ever.

9

From the window Lee watched Des go off down the cart track on an old bike with a basket on the back. He wasn't going to risk going out in the car for he knew that a description of it would have been circulated by the police. He would, in all probability, leave the car in the shed now until he felt the police would have given up looking for it. Or perhaps he would exchange it. He knew how to be patient. Hadn't he waited patiently outside her home until he knew that Brett had left her alone? and then he'd been ready to pounce.

She wondered if it would be possible to unlock the door, and searching round the room, she hoped to find something that might be suitable to pick a lock, but she could find nothing at all. She supposed Des had thought of all that and he'd made quite sure there was no way of escape. It was bad enough being locked in the room when she knew he was there, but to be locked in and completely alone was terrifying. Supposing he had an accident and never came back?

The frustration of being locked in a small room with absolutely nothing to do was terrific. She looked from the window across the most wonderful scenery. On the wooded slopes and rises across the valley she could see an isolated cottage here and there. She could pick out a horse in a field some distance away, cows in another, and lambs. It was agricultural land all around. She supposed prisoners in jail didn't even get a view like this to gaze upon.

She saw a farm lorry moving slowly along a narrow lane a long way away. It would have been nice to be able to walk along those country lanes with some good companions. But not a soul came anywhere near the cottage so there was no chance of calling out to try and tell someone of her plight.

She lay on the bed feeling furious with Des. His talk of loving her was just sickening. How could this be love? She would just be his possession to treat as he wished. Marriage to him would have been a nightmare and because she'd had enough sense to realise this before the marriage took place he was getting his revenge. With him she would never have been able to call her soul her own. He was going to extremes now, she admitted, but a man of his mentality would never have been easy to live with.

It must have been a couple of hours before he returned. It seemed like eternity and she only knew he was back because she could hear him moving about downstairs. She hoped he would be along to unlock the door now that he was back to keep an eye on her and see that she didn't try to escape, but time went on and on and he didn't come. He must be enjoying the feeling of having her locked up like a prisoner. He was letting her see what it had been like for him, he had told her.

Hunger pangs were affecting her stomach, making her feel sick and she thought of the baby she was carrying. She mustn't let any of this affect the child. It couldn't go on for ever. Brett would leave no stone unturned until he had found her she was confident of that. As time went on she wondered if Des was going to deprive her of food to punish her still further.

After what seemed like hours he came up and unlocked the door telling her that if she wanted to go to the bathroom to be quick about it. 'I'm going to fetch you something to eat,' he said.

'Can't I come down for it?' she asked.

'Had enough of being locked up already?' he asked.

'Yes, I have,' she retorted. 'Is this supposed to be the way to prove to me how much you love me?'

'No. It is just to let you see how much I suffered through loving you.'

'You needn't have done,' she said. 'If you had taken the break-up like another man would have taken it you need not have suffered. You have brought misery to yourself, your parents, Roy's family, and now you want to make my life a hell, don't you?'

'When you've been deprived of love as long as I was you'll be glad to turn to me for my love,' he said.

She gasped. 'You mean you'd keep me locked up like a prisoner for years?'

'Depends on you. When you've decided you've had enough and are prepared to give me your love things could be different. Now, if you want to go to the bathroom, go along at once.'

He disappeared downstairs and Lee went off to the bathroom glad of even that little bit of freedom. When she left the bathroom Des came up with a tray of food. There was pork pie, cooked meat, salad and some assorted cakes.'

'I'm going to cook some chops and vegetables later,' he said.

'Let me do it,' she pleaded. 'I can't sit

here any longer just doing nothing.'

He poured her some coffee and told her to get on with her eating. 'My aim is to keep you confined long enough to make you have some sympathy for my having had to spend my life like that. You have shown no sympathy for me at all so far. When I can see that you are prepared to make up to me for my unhappiness I shall give you more freedom. If my plan doesn't work and you feel you cannot give yourself to me as I want you to, I have planned to kill us both and make it look like a suicide pact.'

Her blood ran cold. He spoke so dispassionately, as if killing someone was nothing. 'You wouldn't want Brett to think you'd rather die with me than return to him, would you?' he added.

Lee didn't answer him and tried not to show her fear. That might give him satisfaction. The food he had bought was fresh and appetising and she ate her fill while he sat watching her. Perhaps if she hadn't been carrying the baby within her she would have refused it, but if she refused food herself she would be risking the life of the baby which she hoped and prayed would be delivered safe and sound in her own home with Brett at her side. That was a long way away yet.

It was almost a relief this time when Des collected all the left-overs from the meal and took them to place them outside the door on the floor while he turned the key in the lock. It was unnerving having him sitting there watching her, enjoying the fact that she was his captive.

She wished he would bring her something to read or let her do something to pass the time away. Surely in prison they were not locked up for hours and hours with nothing to do. That was soul-destroying and sadistic.

It was very quiet now. She couldn't hear him moving about and she wondered if he was sitting writing. He was lucky to have found a way of earning a living that satisfied him. He didn't like being with people and so his writing would have given him the pleasure that most people derived from the company of other people. He preferred solitude.

She lay on the bed and slept; there was nothing else to do. How long she slept she had no idea, but she was awoken by the sound of the door being unlocked and she looked up sleepily to see Des standing there.

'I promised to show you some of my illustrations,' he said.

'Oh, yes,' she replied, pushing her hair back from her face, and sitting up.

He sat on the side of the bed and drew her towards him, then he opened a folder and began to show her the pictures he had drawn and explained the story which they were to illustrate. He had drawn a horrific monster of a man which made her shudder. 'Goodness, Des,' she said. 'Will children like anything like that?'

'Of course,' he told her. 'They love to be frightened out of their wits. I used to like reading horrible thrillers when I was young.'

The horrible monster-like man had taken a girl prisoner and she was locked up in a hateful looking castle. The hero was trying to find her having to overcome all sorts of obstacles to reach her. She looked at Des wondering if he was trying to let her see the comparison between her and the girl imprisoned in the castle. Funny how people had enjoyed keeping others in their power, locked in towers, or dungeons, or horrible little cells. Perhaps this sort of literature influenced children and some of them didn't grow out of the fascination it gave them to think of having someone at their mercy even when they became adult. Des was bringing his fantasies into reality. Or was it the other way round in this instance? The drawings were brilliant and yet she hated the evilness of the monster-like man he had portrayed.

'I don't think children should be

filled with this sort of sadistic non-sense,' she said.

'You're wrong. All children like to think of themselves as the hero.

'So you don't like my drawings?'

'I think they're very good. I had no idea you were so talented. It's the theme of your stories I don't like. You make that horrible man so tough and strong which is how boys like to see themselves.'

'I like writing thrillers. I hope I shall write a real spine-chiller one of these days. For adults, not children.'

'I hope you'll be successful, Des. I wondered what you would do when you came out of prison. I thought you might apply for your job back with Lawleys.'

'I never enjoyed that job, although I was successful and drew a good salary. And now I know I can make a living of a sort at writing I shall concentrate on writing all the time.'

'You won't need to make a lot of money living in a place like this.'

'No. You like the cottage?'

'Yes, but you are not giving me a chance to become familiar with it, only this room.'

'There's plenty of time,' he said. 'After a time you'll become attached to the room, you know. I became attached to my cell and preferred to be on my own which wasn't always possible.'

'Weren't you allowed to read, or anything?'

'Maybe I'll let you have something to read, later.'

He gathered up his drawings and left her and she heard that hateful sound once more of the key turning. She had no idea what time it was. She hadn't been wearing her wrist watch when she left the house having taken it off when she had been washing the salad and preparing a snack for herself and Brett. It was awful not even knowing what time it was, but she supposed Des considered that unimportant.

She stood by the window looking longingly across the countryside and

221

suddenly her heart leapt into her mouth when she saw a police car arrive. A couple of policemen were getting out of the car and Brett was there also. Des had heard them too and came dashing up the stairs. She heard him unlocking the door and he looked wild as he came into the room. 'How the hell did they get here?' he asked, as if it were her fault.

'How do I know?' she asked, excitedly.

'Look,' he said, glaring at her fiercely. 'I have this gun and I shan't hesitate to use it and the first to get it will be your husband. If you want to save him you will tell him that you came with me willingly. You are not staying here against your will. You want to stay with me, you understand?'

Her heart was beating like mad. 'Do you understand?' he repeated, urgently, as there were bangs on the door. 'I mean it, Lee. You know I don't make idle threats.'

'Yes,' she whispered.

'Well, give me your hand. Put a smile on your face and convince them that you want to be with me, that we've just come down from making love.'

They went downstairs and Des opened the door and faced the police and Brett. Des looked quite composed. He had his arm around Lee in a friendly way and was so sure of her he knew she wouldn't let him down.

'Lee!' cried Brett, springing forward. 'Lee! Are you all right?'

Des pulled her back from him. 'Of course I'm all right,' she said, giving him a smile. 'I'm sorry I left in such a rush, Brett, I was going to write to you.'

'What?'

'I was going to write and explain that Des came to see me and I knew that I wanted to be with him. I've never stopped loving him in spite of what he did.'

Brett was looking at her dumfounded and she gave him a look, imploring him to go and leave them. She met his eyes and saw the look of incredulity in them, and she tried again. 'I love, Des, Brett. I didn't realise how much until I met him again.'

Brett came towards her again and she put out her hand to stop him. 'No, please, Brett.' She turned to the policemen. 'Please leave us alone. I don't want any trouble. Could you make my husband leave us?'

'If that's what you want, Mrs. Lawley,' they said. 'You might have left a note behind it would have saved us all a lot of trouble. This husband of yours has been out of his mind nearly.'

'I intend to write and explain,' she said, and again gave Brett a look of pleading. 'You must go, Brett. I want to stay here with Des and I don't want there to be any trouble.'

'If that's what you want,' said Brett, in a flat voice, 'that's all there is to it.' He turned to Des. 'Look after her, won't you? Be good to her.'

'Sure,' said Des, with a smile. 'She realises now that she should have waited for me. Should never have given me up in the first place. And as she said, she would have written, and will be writing to make plans for her freedom. She wants to marry me.'

Brett gave Lee one last look and turned away, and the policemen, knowing there was nothing they could do if Lee had left willingly with Des, turned away with him. Lee watched them go, her heart sinking.

'Brett!' she called, in spite of herself, and feeling Des's hold on her strengthen, said, 'I'm sorry,' when Brett turned to look at her, and then Lee went back into the room.

She saw a look of triumph on Des's face as the men left and she knew she was defeated. It was no use praying for help to arrive now for help had come and she had had to pretend she was here willingly with Des. From the window she watched Brett go away.

She turned away despairingly. Why hadn't he protested more? He had left her so easily. She knew she had implored him to go, had wanted him to go so that no harm would come to him, but now that he'd gone she felt devastated.

'Shows how much he thinks of you,' gloated Des. 'I expected him to put up some resistance, but he put up none at all. I killed a man for you,' he bragged. 'And now I have you. You told him you wanted to stay here with me and the police were here as witnesses. Things couldn't have turned out better. The gods are on my side, all right.'

It was too much for Lee, she sank on to a chair and began to cry her heart out. She had been counting so much on Brett and the police finding her. 'That's enough,' said Des, savagely, and gave her a hard slap across the face which startled her so much she stopped crying immediately and looked at him, her eyes drenched in tears. 'That's another way of showing your love,' she scorned.

'Yes. I won't have you crying for another man. Do you hear?'

'I'm crying for my husband,' she said, brokenly.

He pulled her up and shook her. 'You can forget him,' he said. 'He wouldn't lift a finger for you, you saw that.'

What was she going to do? Lee asked herself. She couldn't stay here with Des, and yet there was no one to help her. How could Brett have walked away so easily? Was Des right? Was it true that Brett wouldn't lift a finger for her? Of course he would. The police had told her that he had been out of his mind with worry and she knew that would be true. She must have sounded more convincing than she felt when she told him she loved Des.

'You can get off upstairs,' said Des, 'and get used to the idea that you belong here with me now. Tonight you won't sleep alone. You'll be with me and I'll show you that you are mine.'

He followed her up and imprisoned her in the room again and she flung herself on the bed. If there was some way of killing herself she would. She wouldn't allow him to sleep with her tonight. She wouldn't give him that satisfaction. She belonged to Brett.

But to think of killing oneself is easier than doing it. She knew before she even began to think of ways in which she could do it that she wouldn't. She hadn't the courage.

It got dark early and so there was no longer any point in trying to divert her attention to things happening outside her window. She just sat disconsolately on the side of the bed. She tried to think of ways and means by which she could trick Des into relaxing his watch on her in order that she could get away from him. But what could she do against a man of his strength, and ruthlessness too.

A delicious smell of cooking came wafting up to her and she remembered that he had told her he would be cooking chops later. It wouldn't have hurt him to let her do the cooking as she had offered. At least it would be better than doing nothing for hours on end. She realised how hungry she was and wished she had the strength to refuse food, but she knew if he brought her a nicely cooked meal at this moment she would eat every bit of it. She supposed he had spent some time in this cottage on his own and had taught himself to cook. He wouldn't let her starve to death, for he watched her eat, and she dreaded to think what he'd do to her if she went on a hunger strike, even if she had the strength to do that.

When he came up he looked at her keenly. 'No more tears,' he said, in satisfaction. 'Good! I hope you're going to be sensible now. You can come down for a meal.'

He went off, leaving her to follow at her leisure. She went to the bathroom and tried to make herself look decent. She had her pride and hated to look a mess even in front of Des. Very reluctantly she went down. He said she would get attached to that room and strangely enough she was beginning to feel safer there than downstairs with him.

She hadn't mentioned anything about her pregnancy. If she was forced to live here with him he would learn of her condition and she wondered how he would take that. What would he think about her carrying the baby of another man as he constantly called Brett? He was her husband to be sure, but to Des her husband was not a man to be considered at all. He regarded him with contempt now he knew or thought he knew, that he was a bit of a coward, afraid to put up a fight for his wife.

Des was obviously very pleased with himself as he placed her meal before her. 'Things have turned out so well I can't believe it,' he said, in triumph. 'I never dreamt it would all be so easy.'

'You're enjoying yourself, aren't you? Men who keep a girl against her will are monsters like that man you drew.'

He laughed. 'Lots of women put up resistance in the beginning and it's up to a man to break down that resistance. It all adds to the excitement, and you're right I am enjoying myself. You'll find I'll be quite good to you if you behave yourself.'

'Behave myself, in what way?'

'Well, you have to accept the fact that this is where you belong. I shan't be able to trust you not to try and get away for a long time, but in the end you won't want to leave me.'

What was the use of arguing with him? She was wasting her time. She turned her attention to the meal before her. At least eating was a good way of breaking the monotony for her and the meal was nicely cooked.

'Who taught you to cook?' she asked.

'It's a matter of common sense,' he told her. 'You learn by trial and error.'

'I've been taking cookery lessons,' she said.

'Have you? Perhaps I'll let you try your hand sometime.'

She began to eat and he went on, 'I don't particularly want a family. I would much prefer to have you all to myself. But children would bind you to me. You would stay with me for the sake of the children.'

'You are looking a long way ahead aren't you?' she said coldly.

'I've had lots and lots of time, as I keep reminding you, to plan my way ahead,' he replied. 'How do you think I passed my time away? I used to plan our lives together. Of course I didn't expect you to be married, but that doesn't matter now. Your husband gave you up without the slightest trouble or remorse. How could you love a man like that who cares nothing for you? I thought a woman liked a man to show his mettle and fight for her tooth and nail.'

'How did he know that you were threatening me and him with a gun if I didn't tell him that I loved you?'

'Nothing would stop me from having you.'

'I wish you'd chosen some other woman,' she snapped. 'Somebody who didn't mind being browbeaten. I believe there are some about.'

'I don't want that sort of woman,' he replied. 'I like your spirit, Lee. Your opposition only makes me keener to possess you. I like fighting with you, and I know I shall always win. You're such a tiny thing. I could break you in my two hands.'

'You're mad.'

'Don't try provocation,' he said. 'It won't work. We're going to have a lovely life together with no outside interference. No one has approached this cottage all the time I have stayed here. You could be at the end of the world.'

'No callers at all?'

'The postman, of course, but he won't be seeing you, I'll see to that. I know what time he calls. And then someone from the electricity board will come to read the electric meter and I shall know when they are about to call. No one will be aware that you are living here with me against your will, or not because I shall see that you don't talk to anyone.'

She couldn't believe that anything

like this could really happen. No one would believe that a woman could be compelled to stay with a man in England in this day and age. People would say, 'Surely she could have got away from him and let the police know that she was being held against her will.'

But she had no chance of getting away from him or letting anyone know her plight. She was sure he'd lock her up every time he went out, as people locked up their possessions. And as no one was likely to call she wouldn't be able to attract attention.

Would he allow her to go shopping? she wondered. Not unaccompanied, she knew she couldn't expect that but perhaps he'd take her to the shops to do personal shopping and she could spot her chance. She sounded him out on that. 'Des, I can't live in these clothes indefinitely. I have no change of clothing and I need to change my underwear at least.'

'I'll see to all that for you,' he answered, and as he passed round her to fetch some dessert dishes he stood behind her and put his hands around her bust and began assessing the size of her bra. 'You're bigger than you used to be,' he commented. 'You used to be about thirty-four but I'd say you were thirty-six now.'

She wriggled away from him, angrily, and didn't answer. 'You're not shy of me, surely. We were going to be married, remember?'

She remembered only too well. Remembered how marvellous she had thought he was until she had discovered the flaw in his character. His obssession that she shouldn't talk to any other men, and trying to get her away from everyone she cared for. She supposed if she had married him he wouldn't have kept her a prisoner like this, but her life would have been very restricted. He wasn't normal and perhaps if she had disagreed with his way of living he would have brought her out to a place like this where he could have had complete control over her. And now he declared that she would love him again. That was just wishful thinking on his part. After living with Brett, a decent normal man, she could never love Des again. She would never want anyone else for that matter, but Des least of all.

When the meal was finished and he indicated that she should clear away and wash up. It was almost an order and because activity was better than inactivity she didn't feel so much annoyed at his autocratic way of letting her see that he expected her to do as he ordered. Lee had always been an active person. It was almost a favour being allowed to do something.

When she had finished he went on with his writing and she looked around her. There was no sign of a radio or a television set. He looked up and guessed she was looking for some form of entertainment and said, 'No. I have no radio, no television set. I haven't any time for them. But don't worry, we're going to bed early tonight.'

She felt her inside churning and

prayed desperately that she would escape such a fate. She looked around the room wishing she could see something heavy with which she could hit him hard over the head and he smiled and uncannily seemed to read her thoughts again for he seemed amused. 'You needn't try to do battle with me, Lee, you couldn't possibly win, you know that, don't you. Not a little thing like you.'

It had never bothered Lee before that she was not a very big person and was often referred to as a dainty little piece, but now she wished she was an Amazon type of woman to give Des a run for his money. But of course he wouldn't go for that type of woman. He would prefer someone weak in comparison to himself. He was a coward. But then again, he wasn't. He had killed a man regardless of the consequences.

10

Lee was moving round the room restlessly and Des told her to sit down. 'That's unless you want to go back to your room,' he said. 'I can't concentrate with you distracting my attention.'

He had drawn the curtains, which made them seem so enclosed in this small room after the large sitting-room she was used to in her own home, that it had a claustrophobic effect on her.

'Who does your typing?' she asked.

He frowned at the interruption. 'I take it to an agency.'

Should she offer to do his typing for him? It wasn't that she wanted to do him a favour. It was just that she must have something to do. 'Have you a typewriter?' she asked.

'No. I can't type, anyway.'

'Well, I can. If you had a typewriter I

could soon type your work out for you. It would save you a lot.'

He stopped working and looked at her consideringly. 'You're beginning to see that you'd fit in here with me?'

There was nothing to be gained by antagonising him so she didn't deny it. Supposing she did start doing his typing, and he let her have a go at the cooking, she would soon be behaving exactly as he had intended her to. She would be like a housewife to him and it was either that, or she would be nothing. Just a prisoner until she decided to fall in with his wishes. She could understand now what happened to girls who were forced into marriage. They either had to accept their fate or kick against it and that would get them nowhere. But she was an English girl and didn't have to put up with such a fate, or did she? How was she going to escape it?

Her biggest worry was the thought of having to sleep with him tonight. She couldn't give in to him and dreaded to think what would happen to her if she didn't.

Full of anxiety she watched the minutes ticking away on the wall clock. That would really be the finish, being forced to sleep with him. It was no use telling herself that she had thought of marrying him once and that would have happened naturally, because there was only one man she wanted to make love to her and that was Brett. And she had told Brett that she loved Des, had realised that she'd never stopped loving him. She had been so busy being sorry for herself she had forgotten what Brett was going through. This was his second marriage to fail. What must he be thinking of women at this moment? Perhaps he had believed her so easily because he was used to girls being unfaithful. How she longed to be sitting with Brett instead of in this isolated spot listening to the ticking of that blasted clock which was driving her mad.

It was completely dark outside and

the silence, apart from the clock ticking, was unbearable, but it didn't seem to worry Des. He obviously liked silence as well as solitude.

Lee took a look at the belt of his trousers and there was no sign of the gun. He had put on a jacket when the police came and had held the gun in his pocket. Where had he put it now? He must be feeling more confident knowing that Brett and the police had already been and gone; he was absolutely relaxed, working with great concentration as if she weren't there.

In the silence there came a sound as if someone was moving stealthily outside the cottage. The noise made Lee's heartbeats quicken. If only someone would come, if it was only burglars so that she could take advantage of the diversion to get away. Des heard the noise too and was immediately alert. He went to the window and drew the curtain aside peering out into the darkness. 'Must have been an animal,' he said, 'I can't see anything.'

He hesitated, wondering whether to go outside or not, but it was completely silent again so he thought better of it and turned back to his writing. But after a time he went to fetch the gun out of a bureau drawer and he laid it on the table beside him. 'Can't be too careful,' he said. 'You don't know who may be prowling around.'

'Where did you get that gun?' she asked. 'Isn't it illegal to carry fire arms?'

'You have to be caught carrying them,' he said. 'It wasn't difficult to get it. In jail you meet all types and I met someone who was able to get this for me. I contacted him when I could and I didn't ask any questions as to where he got it from. I paid him well and he was happy so was I.'

'You don't know how many people have been shot with it.'

'No. A good number I should think. It's not particularly new.'

'Have you tried it?'

He looked at her and laughed.

242

'You're hoping it doesn't work? I'm not that daft. I can assure you that I have tried it and it works perfectly. I'm not a bad shot either.'

She began to speak again and he stopped her. 'I wish you'd be quiet. I want to get this finished tonight. The sooner the better.'

She shuddered. The sooner he finished his writing the sooner he would take her to bed with him. He was hateful ordering her to sit quiet like this as if she were a little child. She had a strong feeling that there was someone outside and yet there wasn't a sound. She'd had uncanny feelings that Des had been near her in the past and had tried to dismiss those feelings as just in her imagination, but he had been loitering near, and now she had a very strong feeling that there were human beings outside this cottage. She could feel her heart beating as she kept herself still to concentrate on listening. But Des didn't seem to have any awareness of anything happening and was concentrating on what he was doing. It was just wishful thinking on her part that there was someone outside for the silence continued.

But it didn't continue for long. It was suddenly shattered by the sound of a car starting up. Lee ran to the window as Des sprang to his feet in alarm. The doors of the shed were wide open, she saw as soon as she drew the curtains, and the headlights of the car were full on.

Des came up behind her and exclaimed. 'What the hell! Someone's trying to steal my car.'

He picked up the gun and raced to the door, opened it and dashed outside. She heard the gun go off and followed cautiously behind him to see what was happening. Was this the opportunity she had been looking for? Could she get away while he was involved with the car thieves?

She found herself being caught up in someone's arms and her cry of fright turned to one of joy when she heard

Brett say. 'It's me, Lee. Don't be frightened.'

She turned into his arms and he felt the deep shudders running through her body, and then hearing the gun go off again they both turned to watch the struggle between Des and the police. They were speechless, holding their breath, and suddenly Des gave a groan and slumped to the ground. In the struggle that last shot must have been turned on to Des himself.

They carried him between them into the light of the cottage and one of the policemen turned to Lee and said 'He did it himself. We are not armed. We were trying to take the gun away from him when it went off.'

Des was clutching his side and they saw there was blood on his hand. 'There's no telephone here, is there?' asked one of the officers.

'I'm afraid not,' said Lee, looking at Des, anxiously. 'He needs to be taken to the hospital at once, doesn't he?'

'Can you make it to the car?' Des was asked.

His face was looking rather grey and he muttered. 'Just leave me alone. I don't want to go to the hospital.'

'We must get help for you,' said one of the policemen, not unkindly.

Des turned to Lee. 'Will you come with me?'

'No,' said Brett, sharply. 'She stays with me.'

'But he must be taken to the hospital,' she said, feeling that although she hated Des, she couldn't refuse to help him at this moment. Her prayers had been answered she could afford to be magnanimous. 'You can come too, Brett.'

'You'll have to help yourself to the car,' said a policeman, trying to lift Des. 'You're too heavy to be carried. That's the worst of these isolated spots,' grumbled the officer, 'you can't get help as soon as you'd like. If we got through to the hospital with the help of the car radio and asked them to send an ambulance by the time it got here and then back to the hospital you'd have lost too much blood.'

Des turned to look at Lee and in that moment she felt she didn't hate him any more. She was terribly sorry for him. She went to fetch a large towel which they held close to his side to stop the bleeding while one of the policemen went to fetch the police car which was parked at the end of the track. 'We didn't come up in the car because you can guess we wanted to take him by surprise,' said Brett. 'And everything happened just as we hoped it would. His attention was diverted from you just long enough for me to grab you.'

Lee turned to look at him. 'You didn't believe me when I said I wanted to stay here with him?'

'Of course not, darling. I know you better than that.'

There was no time for any more talk, they just had to concentrate on getting Des to the car. But he protested that he didn't want to go. 'Just leave me alone,' he kept saying.

Already the towel was soaked with blood and they half carried him to the police car. Lee and Brett told him they would follow in his car to the hospital and Lee found herself in tears as she sat beside Brett.

Badly as Des had behaved and relieved as she was to be free of him, she couldn't help feeling sorry for him. Neither Lee nor Brett spoke on the way to the hospital, but Brett at times held out his hand to grip hers tightly and she returned the pressure to let him know how glad she was that he was there at her side, and that she appreciated his sympathy. He knew that she simply couldn't talk about her ordeal, not yet.

When they reached the hospital and had been taken to the waiting room it was then that she saw the signs of strain in Brett's eyes. It seemed that the last few hours had put years on him. Their eyes would meet from time to time and love passed between them without a word being spoken, now wasn't the time for talking.

She saw Des before they took him to the operating theatre to remove the bullet from his side. 'You'll be okay,' she said, trying to give him a smile.

He didn't return her smile. There was such a terrible look of defeat on his face she longed to comfort him. 'He did lift more than a finger for you,' he said, with difficulty, and then he was rushed away.

When they knew there was nothing more they could do Brett had a word or two with the police and then they told him to take Lee to a hotel to get some rest. She thanked them over and over again for rescuing her with tears streaming down her face. 'I thought I was doomed to be kept a prisoner there with him indefinitely,' she said.

'Try and forget it for tonight,' they told her. 'You have your husband to comfort you, and we can talk tomorrow.'

As soon as they were alone in their

hotel room Brett took her in his arms and they clung to each other. 'You don't know what I've been through,' he said, huskily. 'It's been like a nightmare thinking of you at the mercy of that madman.'

'Brett, he didn't, he didn't do anything, you know.'

'Thank God. I was afraid to ask that.'

'He kept me locked in a bedroom most of the time. He thought he was going to keep me a prisoner there and that I would learn to love him again. And I was beginning to believe he was going to get away with it after you'd arrived with the police and then left again.'

'We guessed he was armed and it's no use being brave at the risk of losing your life, that wouldn't have done you any good.'

'It was agony for me to have to tell you to leave me with him, but I knew he intended to use that gun if he was thwarted in his intentions. He told me I had to convince you that I loved him and went with him willingly, otherwise he was going to shoot you.'

'Oh, my darling. You were marvellous. But we weren't fooled. We guessed why you said you wanted to stay. He had one arm around you and the other hand he had in his pocket obviously covering a weapon. And if you could have seen your face, love. The pupils of your eyes were dilated with fear, and when you implored me to leave you it was the hardest thing in the world to do, but I knew that was the best thing to do: pretend we believed you, and then take him by surprise.'

The waiter brought them drinks and Brett insisted that Lee had a good strong drink. 'You need it,' he said, 'and I think I need a stiff drink too.'

'Des never suspected that it might be you and the police returning,' she said, when the waiter had gone. 'He was convinced that someone was trying to steal his car, and it's a new one. He went out and fired his gun without hesitation. It might have been some young kids stealing his car, for we know they do, and that they shouldn't, but to fire at them . . . he could have killed again.'

'I suppose when a man has killed once he's got no compunction about killing again. It wouldn't worry Des whether it was a youngster or not. Roy was little more than a youngster and he killed him in cold blood.'

'Who thought of pretending to steal the car?'

'Oh, that was my brainy idea, but the police wouldn't let me take a great part in the deception. They thought it a good idea, but they broke into the shed and started the car up. They told me to keep in the background and take care of you when I could.'

'We heard a noise and Des looked through the window to see if he could see anything but it was black outside and he said he thought it was an animal, but he kept his gun handy after that.'

'Yes, we saw the light from the

window when he drew the curtain aside and looked out. We crouched down against the wall and held our breath while he was looking but should have known that although we could see him in the lighted window, he couldn't see us in the dark. We expected him to come out then and that would have been tricky, but we were prepared to be confronting an armed man and we would have had more chance in the dark for he wouldn't have known which direction to fire in.'

'I sensed there was someone out there, but Des was quite unconcerned until he heard his car start up.'

'Most men think a lot of their car and we thought that would take him by surprise and get him in a tizz, thinking someone was taking it away from him.'

'How did you find the cottage?'

'Well, that was a stroke of luck. When I went to the police they gave out a call for people to watch out for your car, naturally, and then we went round to his parents' home to ask them where he could be.'

'I'll bet they were terribly upset. They're a nice couple.'

'Yes, it's a shame for them. They were very helpful. Mrs. Palmer was terribly worried over you, Lee, in case he should harm you. She said her son had been acting strangely and secretively and she was afraid. They knew he had bought a cottage somewhere, but he hadn't told them where and they thought that was strange.'

'Do you think they were afraid of him?'

'No, I think they were more afraid of what he might do. His father helped us to look through all his belongings. We were looking for something to give us a clue as to where the cottage was. We thought there might be some papers containing the address, or something to do with the transaction, the name of the estate agents he had contacted for instance, but he had covered his tracks very thoroughly. There was absolutely nothing in any of his drawers or in his bedroom . . . and then we had a break. There is always some little thing that can be overlooked. His father found the clue. It was a phone number on a piece of paper near to the telephone directory. A strange number to him and Mrs. Palmer and so the police checked it out and it belonged to a firm of estate agents.'

'He'll kick himself when he knows he left that clue behind.'

'It's always something simple that can give people away. All the papers to do with the transaction had been taken away. By the time we got that clue the evening was nearly over but it wasn't long before we could get in touch with the agent who informed us that they had sold a cottage but to a Mr. Simkiss who had paid for it in cash. It hadn't been a great amount because the place needed such a lot of renovation.'

'And you had no doubt that Mr. Simkiss was the name used by Des.'

'Well, it seemed too much of a coincidence for it not to have been Des

Palmer. He'd bought a cottage recently and that estate agent's number was there so he must have been in touch with him, and he obviously bought it under an assumed name to cover up tracks of his whereabouts and then unwittingly left that telephone number to give us a clue.'

'He had been making plans for a long time to pick me up and keep me there. He was amazed when he saw you and the police. He couldn't think how you'd got to know where he was, and then he was absolutely delighted when he thought you'd taken it in that I was with him quite willingly, and was sure he'd got away with it and could keep me with him for good. He said the police were witnesses that I had said I wanted to stay there with him.'

'He'll have plenty of time to think what a fool he was, for it's back to jail for him without a doubt.'

Lee looked troubled. 'I do wish it hadn't happened. I think he needs to be put in a mental home rather than a jail.'

Neither Brett nor Lee could get to sleep when they went to bed for they kept thinking of something else to tell each other. Lee told Brett that Des had threatened to kill her and himself if she didn't return his love after a time. 'He said he would make it look like a suicide pact. That was to hurt you. To make you believe that I would rather die with him than return to you.'

'He couldn't have hoped to get away with it even if we hadn't found that vital clue,' said Brett. 'The police would have found him if they'd had to search every cottage in the country, and I'd have been helping them.'

'That's what I kept telling myself,' said Lee, 'but when you actually came and I had to send you away again I felt shattered. But if I hadn't obeyed his orders you'd have been dead now, Brett.'

'We knew we had to proceed with caution,' said Brett. 'The police were aware that he was a murderer and admit now that his sentence hadn't been long enough. He shouldn't have been at large to threaten you again.'

'Perhaps they'll lock him away for good now,' said Lee, but the thought only depressed her. And yet if he was given another short sentence she would still be afraid when he was released again.

Brett seemed to know how she was feeling and they lay there in each other's arms, not wanting to go to sleep, and too upset to make love. They were so very thankful that she was safe and apparently no harm had come to the baby for the following morning Lee was plagued as usual with morning sickness.

After breakfast Lee asked Brett if he would mind ringing the hospital to find out how Des was. 'You're not worrying over him, are you?' he asked.

'Well, I can't help wondering whether he was seriously injured. It was his own fault, I know, and it could have been someone else quite innocent who got shot, but I can't help feeling a bit sorry for him.'

Brett went off and returned to say that Des had had an operation to remove the bullet and was satisfactory. He was having blood transfusions to make up for loss of blood.

'Can we go home, or will the police want to talk to us?' she asked.

'I should think we can go home,' said Brett. 'You'll be wanted to give evidence against Des when he recovers, but that won't be for some time. I'll find out if it's okay for us to leave.'

A policeman came round, took a few notes and told them they wouldn't be needed again for the time being. 'Can I use Des's car to get us back home?' asked Brett. 'He won't be needing it for a bit.'

'Yes, that will be okay. You can leave it at his parent's address.'

And it was only when Lee was back in their own home that she felt she could relax after the nightmare she had been through. She went all through the house just to convince herself that she was really back home safe and sound, and Brett stayed with her as if afraid to leave her side.

Everyone they knew wanted to see her, having heard of what had happened. There was her own family and Brett's family, their friends all wanting her to know how glad they were to know that she was safely back home. All these people meant so much to her and it was good to know they cared. The love of one's family and friends is so precious and Des wanted her to sacrifice all that. If he had his way she wouldn't have seen any of them again.

'I'll never, never take anything for granted again, Brett,' she said. 'If I never knew how much I loved you before I do now.'

'I never took you for granted, Lee. I knew how lucky I was to have you after my first disastrous marriage. When I returned and discovered you were not in the house I knew what had happened and was absolutely frantic. I knew that wicked devil had taken you away and I

260

was so afraid for you. Every minute we were apart was like a year.'

It was an ordeal that they couldn't put out of their minds quickly, but in Brett's arms Lee began to feel safe again. 'I feel as if I've escaped from something evil,' she told him.

'If he had touched you I'd have killed him myself, I'm sure,' said Brett.

Within the next few days Lee went to see her doctor who confirmed that she was having a baby and that everything was in order. Of course there had never been any doubt about it, but Brett was very thrilled to have it confirmed. He stayed away from work for a few days to be with her until her nerves had settled down to normal. 'I couldn't concentrate on work anyway,' he said. 'My own nerves haven't settled yet. We've had such a fright, darling.'

And together they settled down again to their happy-go-lucky way of living once more. Brett began to tease her again and she responded with laughter and retaliation. They were back to normal.

Then they heard some news which shocked Lee, although she would now have peace of mind in the future. The police came to tell them that Des had escaped from the hospital, in spite of police supervision at the hospital. But he had tricked them and not only had he been able to get away from the hospital, but he had also managed to get hold of some dangerous drugs. He had been found not far from the hospital after taking the drugs and was suffering from exposure after having been lying out in a field all night. He had been taken back to the hospital and had failed to recover consciousness.

'There will have to be an enquiry, of course,' said the policeman. 'But he was very crafty. He planned his escape quite well, and he obviously intended to take his own life.'

'Hey, what's this?' cried Brett, when he saw the tears streaming down Lee's face.

'It's stupid, isn't it? I could never have had any peace while he was alive, unless he was locked away, and I didn't wish that on him. But it seems so tragic. He brought all this trouble on himself and made life hell for others too. His poor Mum and Dad have suffered so much because of him. He was their only son. I think I should go and see them.'

Brett held her close to him sympathetically and she remembered that hard slap Des had given her across the face when he had seen her in tears. She dried her eyes and said, firmly, 'I won't cry for him.'

Instead she began to enjoy life as she hadn't been able to enjoy it for a long time because the shadow of Des had been hanging over her ever since she'd decided not to marry him. She was lucky to have found a man like Brett and wouldn't let him see her upset.

Brett no longer need be afraid to leave her alone in the evening or any other time now for fear that Des might come along and yet for all that he still wanted to remain near to her. He wouldn't go out at night unless she was going with him, and Lee knew how he felt because she was always happiest when he was near.

'Brett, I'm so happy,' she would exclaim, for no reason at all.

And he, understanding, would take her in his arms and kiss her. 'I'm very happy too,' and Lee knew that with the wrong man life could be hell, but with the right man it could be heaven. And Brett was the right man for her.

They would have their good times and a few bad, no doubt, but never again would she have to live under the cloud of Des's jealousy and possessiveness. Lee hoped he was at peace, and thanked God for the peace and happiness she had with her wonderful Brett.

We do hope that you have enjoyed reading this large print book.

Did you know that all of our titles are available for purchase?

We publish a wide range of high quality large print books including:
Romances, Mysteries, Classics
General Fiction
Non Fiction and Westerns

Special interest titles available in large print are:
The Little Oxford Dictionary
Music Book, Song Book
Hymn Book, Service Book

Also available from us courtesy of Oxford University Press:
Young Readers' Dictionary
(large print edition)
Young Readers' Thesaurus
(large print edition)

For further information or a free brochure, please contact us at:
Ulverscroft Large Print Books Ltd.,
The Green, Bradgate Road, Anstey,
Leicester, LE7 7FU, England.
Tel: (00 44) **0116 236 4325**
Fax: (00 44) **0116 234 0205**

Other titles in the
Linford Romance Library:

CONVALESCENT HEART

Lynne Collins

They called Romily the Snow Queen, but once she had been all fire and passion, kindled into loving by a man's kiss and sure it would last a lifetime. She still believed it would, for her. It had lasted only a few months for the man who had stormed into her heart. After Greg, how could she trust any man again? So was it likely that surgeon Jake Conway could pierce the icy armour that the lovely ward sister had wrapped about her emotions?